KU-049-849

CONTENTS

NOT MY STORY

Jane De Suza

This is the weird thing about this story.

I am not writing it.

Seriously. I'm not. Seriously – I wish I could stop saying that, because it's a funny story sometimes actually. So the thing is I'm not saying the 'seriously' bit because. I. Am. Not. Writing. This.

Let's start earlier.

Let's start that evening after school a few days back, when I was actually writing something. One hundred lines on how I would be good in class. Except I was writing that at home. And no one should have to work at home, you'll agree. That's just really unfair. And our Science teacher, Kushal

Sir was really unfair. Just because Nandu and I were sharing a joke he was not supposed to see on his dad's WhatsApp, Kushal Sir roared at both of us, and he asked Nandu to tell the whole class what we were talking about. So, of course, Nandu told the joke he was not supposed to see, and Kushal Sir turned red and screamed at us both, and gave us those hundred lines on being good and not looking at jokes we're not supposed to see and not talking in class and listening to elders yada yada yawn. The line itself was like a para.

Well, as I was writing it, I looked out of the window of our apartment on the first floor, and I saw Khoo, my little sister trying to ride my brand new cycle downstairs in the open grassy patch in front of our apartment. Khoo, which is short for Khushnam, has a cupboard full of her own silly toys but always takes mine.

'Hey!' I shouted. 'Hey you! Khoo! Yoo hoo!' It didn't work.

So, since I was not allowed to leave the house (mom's rules) until I finished my hundred lines about listening to elders etc., and she had locked the door, I decided to slip over the balcony railing (which I've done a million times before), and get my cycle back. And as I was dangling there, holding onto the grill, and looking (Pawan told me later) like a pyjama on a string, Khoo came cycling past, wobbling and grinning at me cheekily. Grrr! I tried to kick out at her, and grab at her hair at the same time, but of course, not being a Russian acrobat, my hands and legs don't coordinate like that.

And so I fell.

On my right arm. And I broke it. And I yelled so hard, Khoo slammed the cycle into a lamp post in fright. And all the pigeons flew away. And my mom came running to look over the balcony, and almost fell over herself, so frightened was she to see her son with a broken arm, and her daughter with a broken cycle.

Then, many helpful neighbours took me to the hospital, while I cried and sobbed, and didn't act like a big boy at all (I'm eleven, by the way). I'm big when I want to sleep late and I'm big when I want to go out alone to the corner shop, but I'm small when something is hurting and I want my mom to make it go away.

Khoo too was crying and sobbing and because she is only seven and cute with little fountain pigtails, the doctors and nurses were all fussing over her, though she had only one tiny scratch on her knee and I had a broken arm. BROKEN ARM, people! Look here!

Dr. Bannerjee looked at the X-ray of my arm and said, 'Now Cyrus, how did you go break your arm, young man?'

'It broke because I had to write a hundred lines. You really should get my teacher arrested.' (Can't say I didn't try).

Dr. Bannerjee seemed to think this was funny. He wiped his eyes and began, 'Luckily ...'

Luckily? What was lucky about breaking my arm, breaking my new cycle, being punished – all on one stupid day?

'Luckily,' said Dr. Bannerjee, 'we have just received a new experimental plaster. And I am going to use it on you, you lucky young man. It is made of new generation healing material, and moulds itself to the patient's arm, is flexible and yet firm. It controls your arm perfectly. In fact, it is so efficient, it's practically alive.'

And so I went home with the plaster cast which was long and yellow and smelled awful and was practically—alive—hah! While Khoo went home with cute Barbie plasters and a lollipop to make her stop crying.

'Now Cyrus, no using your arm, remember,'

said my mom and then as strange as only adults can be – told me to complete my imposition of hundred lines.

'How? I'm not supposed to. Use. My. Arm.'

'Write with your other hand,' said my mom, patting my head. 'Write those lines about how you must listen to elders. In fact, I feel like adding one more line. About how not to go jumping off balconies.'

Ha, very funny. Seriously. (I did not write that. Wait, wait.)

So there I was, with my right arm, which is my 'write-arm' in a sling. I had so many other questions. Like, how would I you know, wash myself after a—you know—and all that.

* * *

Now pay attention. Because here's when it starts to get creepy.

Through the grumbling, I started to write with my left hand, and then my right hand shot out, plaster and all, and grabbed the pen. But did it write the lines?

No way. It began to scribble on my open book. It made a funny face. Then it made a funny face with a scratchy moustache and glasses. Oh no, it was drawing Kushal Sir. Stop! But I couldn't stop my hand. It went on drawing Kushal Sir, and then—hey, it drew a speech blurb coming out of his mouth—saying, 'No joking, no talking, no laughing, no nothing.'

I took my eraser in my left hand and began to erase the sketch, and my right arm knocked the eraser right out of the window. Seriously!

I'd lost control of my arm. How? All that stupid Khoo's fault.

I told my mom I was in intolerable pain and I wanted dinner in my room. She agreed and brought me a tray with lots of food. I didn't really feel like eating any, I was in a morose mood. So, it was fine when my right arm grabbed the parathas and flung them out of the window. Not me, get it. The arm in the 'practically alive' plaster.

Of course! It was the plaster—it was a weird, demoniac thing—it had a life of its own. It was making my arm do stuff it never should.

I fell asleep, staring hard at the plaster. And woke next morning with a slap to my face. Ouch! My mom had never done that before. But my mom wasn't even in my room. While I looked unbelievingly at my right arm, it slowly raised itself and was about to give my cheek another slap when I shouted, 'I'm awake, no more!' It stopped. Whoa!

* * *

The next few days were, as you can imagine, stranger than a hippo driving a scooter in Antarctica.

In the beginning, I was a class hero, what with the new yellow plaster cast.

'How did you break it?' Everyone wanted to know.

I might have, you know, bent the truth a bit. I told them how I had rescued a pigeon from a kite string on a tree branch dangling from a phone wire on a lamppost ... as my story gathered wings, I had reached the point when I was fighting off attacking crows all alone ... when the bell rang, and class began.

Over the day, everyone wanted to sign on my plaster cast. Nandu drew a big smiley face on the forearm. Some kids drew hearts and crosses and cricket balls etc. Joey tried drawing a pigeon but it looked like a brinjal with a beak.

Of course, things didn't go so smoothly. In fact, they went completely crazy.

At lunchtime, the senior class bully, Shirish,

wandered over to help himself to whatever he felt like from our lunch boxes. He was like that. He had three other Neanderthal morons who followed him around and the best of our lunch— puris, rasagollas, pizzas—all went to these guys.

Shirish swaggered over and raised his eyebrows at me. 'Oh look here, poor little Cyrus has an itsy-bitsy boo-boo on his arm. He must have cried like a baby.'

Nandu said, 'He didn't. He saved birds and fought off—er—other birds.'

Shirish laughed. 'Did he really? Well, how kind. I'm sure he won't mind sharing his sandwich with me then.'

And then to my horror, my right hand fixed its fingers around a sandwich from my lunchbox, opened it up and slapped it right across Shirish's shocked face. The buttery side. He stood there with scrambled egg dripping down his nose, while there was a burst of laughter, which quickly subsided after he glared at everyone.

Then, turning back to me, he roared like an angry bull and lunged at me. Of course, we'd all seen it coming and so took off as fast as our legs could go.

* * *

We managed to stay out of Shirish's way for a couple of days, looking around corners of corridors and posting guards at the stairs and stuff like that. But my plaster misbehaved like a tantrum-throwing three-year-old.

It spun parathas like a Masterchef and then flung them around, it threw pencils like darts at the wall, it drummed on the desk when the teacher's back was turned, and kept reaching out to everyone else's lunch boxes and stuffing food into my mouth.

Soon, I was not a hero any more.

The other kids gave me either angry or scared looks and quickly turned away when I hopped cheerfully into class. And after my plaster-cast hand pulled Khoo's pigtails and she went crying to my mom, I was on the blacklist at home too. Other things happened at home as well, which I'm not telling you – things like my mom's dupatta being flung at the fan, and her shoe being put into the fish tank (quickly retrieved, thankfully, for the fish).

'What is wrong with you, Cyrus?' my mom kept asking. 'Why are you being even more difficult nowadays? You know that Daddy being away on the ship forces me to work doubly hard to bring you both up. I don't think he'd be very happy to know what you're up to.'

I worshipped my dad, and felt even worse. I didn't want to upset him. I hung my head.

Mom's tone changed. 'Is there something wrong? Oh my gosh, did you fall on your head too, that day?'

'No, no,' I said miserably. Then I decided to tell my mom about the plaster cast. I mean, she was a sweet person and worked so hard, as she'd just said.

Guess how well that turned out?

Right!

Not well at all!

'It's this new plaster cast,' I started. 'It's got a mind of its own. It's evil. It makes me do things like—naughty things—it makes me get into trouble. It keeps throwing stuff around, and I can't help it.'

My mom looked at me with surprise written all over her face. 'Cyrus, please don't talk nonsense. You need to have the courage to tell the truth.'

'It's the truth. Seriously. I have another week left to take off this plaster cast. Before that, it's going to act so bad, it's going to get me murdered.'

FUNNY STORIES

'Such exaggeration, really!' My mom shook her head, quite annoyed, and walked off. 'Couldn't think of anything else to blame it on except a non-living thing – a plaster cast, for goodness sake, which is helping you get better.'

'It's not non-living, didn't you hear the doctor?' I yelled after her. 'It's practically alive. It's alive. As alive as you or me, though it may kill me soon.'

The plaster cast made my arm shoot out and send my skate rolling across the floor after my mom. She turned around and snapped at me. 'That's it. No more TV, no more video games all week. They're giving you an over-active imagination. You're grounded!'

I stared after her, horrified. Then glared at the plaster. 'Look what you've done!' I wailed.

And remember that smiley face that Nandu had drawn on it? I swear—it winked at me—that face. That blue gel-pen-drawn face – it closed one eye deliberately and slowly, and then it widened its stupid grin at me.

I began to whack at it, but of course, that only hurt my own arm more, so I stopped.

* * *

11

I thought I'd spend the last week in bed, but my mom suddenly wised up to my tummy-pains as bad as 'galloping horses' and my throat hurting like a 'desolate desert'. The more poetic and more painful my symptoms got, the funnier she found them.

And so, I went off to school, and the plaster cast made me do things that made me shrink in shame. It pulled people's hair and flung lunchboxes around. Then, on the way home, while passing the sandbox where the little kids play, it actually took my bag and dragged it through a sand-castle some toddlers were building.

That did it of course. The toddlers cried like they all had broken arms instead of broken sandcastles. Their teacher came rushing over and then all the teachers got their heads together in the staff room and I was hauled to the Principal's office.

'It is a disciplinary issue, Cyrus,' the Principal boomed. 'This is a highly respectable school and we do not condone such rowdy behaviour. This is your last warning. The next time, you will be suspended.'

My right arm shot out and wiggled its fingers over my nose. No, no, no!

The Principal couldn't believe his eyes. He took off his glasses and wiped them clear and looked at me again. My plaster cast was now forcing my hand to sweep everything off his table.

'Good gracious!' he exclaimed. 'I think the boy has gone quite mad. I think our school counsellor should be seeing him.'

Of course, after my right arm pulled my school counsellor's tie so hard, it almost choked him, he decided he didn't want to see me.

'It's my plaster cast,' I kept protesting to them all. 'It's not me. It's my plaster cast that's making my arm do all that. Seriously. It's practically alive.'

The counsellor told the Principal and teachers and my mom that I was using my plaster cast as an excuse. 'This is what this child has always wanted to do. All this mischief. This plaster has given him an excuse to carry it out.'

No, no, no! Of course, no one believed me, and a very disappointed mom took me home.

Then came the last day – the day before the plaster was finally to come off. Thank all the stars and gods and medical journals and pigeons (I even felt like hugging Khoo), I was so relieved.

But the last day was a day out of hell. Because Shirish was finally waiting for me, and since I was so mopey, I was not on guard, and he jumped out from behind the water-cooler and caught my collar. Then he marched me outside. 'Now, let's settle this,' he smirked.

A crowd of kids quickly built up around us once we were outdoors. 'Put up your fists and fight like a man, Cyrus,' said Shirish, who was of course, built like a rhino. 'Or can you only fight birds? Hahaha.'

So I dolefully put up my fists and then, my right arm went ballistic. It shot out and stunned everyone, including me. And stunned Shirish more than once, of course. It boxed like a pro. It punched Shirish in the nose, and got him in the gut, and slapped his cheek so there was a red mark across his shocked face.

Slowly, the crowd of kids who had been bullied for years, began to cheer. Though I was growing paler and paler. I was going to be killed for this, for sure. But then, a strange thing happened. My right arm raised itself again – and Shirish crouched back, holding his palms up. 'Don't, don't! I give up. I'll never bother you again, I promise. Leave me alone.'

'Or my friends,' I said (just gave it a shot, you know).

'Or your friends,' he agreed. 'Please don't hit me again.'

I was so surprised I was ready to leave it at that. But that rowdy old plaster-cast right arm began to go for him again. And Shirish turned and ran. At least, he tried to run. But, he tripped over someone's toe, and crashed to the floor so awkwardly, he began to howl.

And guess how it all ended?

The next day, my plaster cast was taken off by Dr. Bannerjee, as promised. I winked at it, and that face that Nandu drew, winked back, I swear. It was kind of bitter-sweet.

But I'm saving the best part for last (and yeah, this is ME writing this now – me of my own will and my own hand). Dr. Bannerjee said in parting, 'Since this plaster was so successful for you, Cyrus, we've decided to use the experimental plaster on another boy from your school. A boy who broke his leg yesterday. A boy called Shirish.'

SUNDAY RAT

Chatura Rao

*T*he rat stood stiff as a statue in the middle of the crowd that jostled to reach him. He was a huge silver fellow with standing up ears and a collar around his neck, also in silver, all beautifully carved with flowers and birds. 'Like that makes up for having to act like a statue day in and day out,' Mooshaka silently grumbled. 'And then there is that business of Wishes. Here it comes now!'

The first devotee of the evening elbowed her way through the crowd. She leaned over his back, putting her great weight across him as she shut his right ear with her plump right palm and whispered loudly in his left: 'I want my daughter to marry that Navani boy. Make sure it comes through properly. And we cannot afford a destination wedding, so mind that—'

'Move over aunty, you've had your turn!' a young man nudged impatiently.

'Okay, okay. Young people these days always in a hurry,' aunty grumbled, waddling towards Orange's sanctum. Orange was the main deity of this temple. However, Mooshaka, the silver rat, was just as popular.

'Holy Rat, India has to reach the Super Eight of the Saucer Cup,' the young man said. 'I've bet 20,000 rupees on this. Please make it happen.' He sauntered over to fold his hands before Orange. Orange was hard of hearing and only the rat could squeak in a frequency that Orange would understand. So every night as Mooshaka bore his master back to Mount Kailash to sleep beside his divine parents, the divine rat had the long and tiring task of conveying the devotees' wishes to his master. A master who often incredulous.

'WHAT?! The Navani boy! O Shiva, father-in-heaven, why would anybody want to marry their daughter to that pot-bellied wart?!' Orange would exclaim. 'Not that a big belly is bad or anything,' he would mutter, lovingly patting his own.

'And India reach the Supersix? Super What? Supereight? That isn't even as good as Supersix! Anyway, even if *Superman* played cricket for India the team would not reach the Super Eight! How am I supposed to grant impossible wishes? Just the other day, a man asked me to grant him a grandson. The man has neither a son nor a daughter to begin with. Ha!'

Mooshaka would shrug and simply carry on listing the devotees' wishes. He hated them. The devotees had no sense and were greedy and ... and their armpits often smelt like soggy socks when they leaned over! Still Orange insisted on hearing all their wishes and even tried to grant about half of them.

All Mooshaka wanted was a break. Conveying the wishes was one thing. The other (worse) thing was that his master was getting almost too fat to carry over the cold clouds to the distant peaks of Mount Kailash. Orange would have to hire a camel soon if he didn't stop pigging out on the laddoos every night. Mooshaka wanted to take no more requests, just run away to where nobody recognised his divine squeaking powers and silver carved collar. He just wanted, for once in his life, to enjoy life as an ordinary guy.

* * *

'I won't.' One Saturday Mooshaka crouched under a bench in the empty temple after closing hours. 'I simply won't. I'm on strike. *Dukaan band.*'

He was a rat of few words, and Orange who actually really loved him, immediately sat down to negotiate slave rights. 'Hmmph,' he blew through his elephant trunk. 'You want to take a holiday. But where will you go?'

'Send me somewhere fun.'

'Kulu Manali for white water rafting? Auli for skiing?'

Mooshaka shook his head: 'Where do the devotees go on Sunday?'

'The shopping malls.'

'What are they called?'

'Infinite mall, In Orbit mall, I forget the rest …' Orange said, racking his memory, but he just couldn't recall more because he was poor at names the way he was hard of hearing.

'Send me to In Orbit mall. I would like to go *into orbit* for a day. Should be divine,' Mooshaka said dreamily.

Orange almost pointed out that Mount Kailash touched the stars and *was* divine, but he was a kind god and of course, granter of wishes, so he just nodded. 'Tomorrow you will be transformed into a human being and will find yourself at the entrance of In Orbit mall. Good night.'

Orange whistled sharply. A camel appeared before them swimming a few inches above the ground, his legs waving slowly, hump quivering, mouth contentedly chewing the cud. Before Mooshaka could be properly stunned, could properly realise that Orange could actually read his mind, the rotund god boarded the camel's back. The camel's eyes widened at the weight. He looked despairingly at Mooshaka, beast-of-burden to beast-of-burden, who smiled slightly and waved, 'See you!' Orange sunk his heels into the camel's back, yanked at the reigns and called 'Hurrrr.' Then Orange and the camel disappeared.

Mooshaka awoke the next day to find himself standing on the long, shiny steps of the In Orbit mall. Someone was holding him by the hand. Someone taller than him and fatter too. It was the plump aunty who visited the temple every

Tuesday! Mooshaka looked down at himself. He was a very short boy, about eleven years old, and he was plump. He had a twitchy long nose and a bit of a moustache. His teeth were protruding, though he wore braces to correct them.

Mooshaka looked down. Red shoes, blue pants and a white shirt with a buttoned-up collar that had designs of flowers and birds. A collar, even here. His heart sank. 'Oh Orange, why can't I be free on my one holiday?' The top buttons of the tight collar promptly popped off and free he was!

'Come, come, my dear grandson,' the aunty said, yanking him up the steps. 'Let's have fun in our usual Sunday way.'

'Our usual way?' Mooshaka ventured timidly.

'Yes, dumb chokro!' aunty exclaimed. 'Eat eat eat. Play play play. How can you forget our favorite motto?'

'Eat and play? Yes, of course I remember,' said Mooshaka leaping up the stairs in excitement. He dragged the huffing-puffing aunty behind him. 'I had forgotten on account of studying so hard all week!'

'Studying? You?' Aunty gasped with laughter. 'That'll be the day!'

They took the elevator to the second floor which was the food section. Here aunty suggested Mooshaka have a pizza, while she ate chaat. The rat-boy nodded eagerly, his plump chin bobbing. He was hungry for his breakfast, which was usually upma or poha at the temple.

But when the pizza came, Mooshaka was transported—you guessed it—to high heaven. He was a rat who had never tasted cheese! *Never ever.*

The pizza was covered with thick, warm, stringy cheese. Mooshaka ate it quickly and asked for one more, but aunty, who was his grandmother in this scenario, just would not buy him another. She said that he had diabetes, and that strange word rung a bell. Three Tuesdays ago at the temple, aunty had whispered in Mooshaka's ear that her grandson, Jignes, had juvenile diabetes and to please make him well. 'So that is who I am!' Mooshaka realised. 'Jignes.'

Well, who cared about the fellow and his problems? Mooshaka was on his first holiday in 2000 years and he wanted cheese! 'Gimme more!' Mooshaka shouted in his mind, knowing not to say it to aunty. So, indicating that he had to visit the washroom, Jignes-Mooshaka slipped into the kitchen of Pizza Palace. He scurried about in rat fashion, knees bent, his hands hooked in front of his chest, nose thrust forward sniffing. He did not notice how the cooks stopped to stare at him like he was crazy. And then he came upon it: a fourteen-inch pizza with layers and layers of cheese melting on it, still warm from the oven.

Outside in the restaurant of Pizza Palace, aunty was starting to worry. Where was her grandson? It had been ten minutes since he'd said he had to go to the Men's Room. That too he had indicated by pointing to a place roughly below his tummy and then had trickled a glass of water on the floor. Really! Jignes' communication skills were going from bad to worse. 'I will just have to take this up with Rupa,' she said huffily to herself, Rupa being Jignes' mother. 'She does nothing but go to kitty parties all day. What will become of the boy? He is not fit for human company!'

Dhaam dhoom! Pisk-Posk! Clang BANG! Sounds of battle from the kitchen interrupted her thoughts as well as the happy munching of other pizza eaters. '*Su che* ...?' Aunty started to say in her native language, but was shut up by an awful sight at the kitchen door.

Jignes, on seeing the cheesy pizza, had rushed towards it. In his path were two cooks, one with a plate of chopped capsicum and the other with a big bowl of pasta sauce. Jignes barged straight through. The chef at the other end of the kitchen, who had been keeping a suspicious eye on Jignes, walked into a steel tray of spaghetti, which slipped into a pile on the floor and made a waiter (also busy staring at the boy nosing around the kitchen) slip and fall against another, who fell against another, until all the kitchen help had gone down like skittles in a bowling alley.

As the pile of moaning and cursing cooks dusted themselves off and tried to get up, Jignes passed among them like a young god passing through the muck of the world. He picked up the pizza of his dreams and messily gobbled half by the time he reached the kitchen door.

The sight that greeted his grandmother's eyes was that of plump, diabetic Jignes pigging out on layers and layers of crusty, forbidden cheese. 'O! Orange! Save my grandson from his madness!' Aunty cried.

Orange, who was at this moment reclining on his temple throne eating a huge modak after his huge mid-day meal, heard her prayer. You do remember that he was hard of hearing and needed Mooshaka to convey his devotees' requests? Perhaps he had been fooling himself all those years, for he heard her quite clearly. Uttering a few magic words which sounded like 'Clang BANG' to the uninitiated (and unimaginative), he transformed Mooshaka into ...

Zweeep Vion VIONN! Mooshaka was at the bike racing video game. He had become Tejasvini, the video game whiz kid. Teju was a chewing gum addict too, so she was not interested in eating anything at the food court. She was instead busy winning game after game. Until Mooshaka became her. Then Teju suddenly assumed a posture like a jungle rat caught in the headlights of a car, and froze at the video game controls. Her onscreen bike went out of control and crashed into the railing of the race track, throwing the driver off and beginning to catch fire.

'Come on, Teju!' 'What's the matter with you?!' Teju's cousins Sunil and Misha screamed. Mooshaka-Teju came to her senses. She wildly pressed the controls until she saw her screen self run for the fallen bike, right it and jump on. Then Mooshaka-Teju raced it better than the real Teju. Even better, because being a divine rat, she always knew what was going to happen next. She knew when the blue bike would swerve into her path and she knew when the yellow bike rider would pick up speed and catch up with her to kick her bike down. So she did not allow these pre-designed moves. She beat the video game, thrashed it, winning one race after another, losing no points at all. A crowd gathered around Mooshaka-Teju, her hair flying out behind her as she attacked the game board at a crazy speed. Then the video game monitor suddenly went blank and the machine began to wail loudly, like a monster baby crying.

All the kids around her and at the other games jumped in horror at the sound of the machine giving up the fight. The wail sounded like an enemy plane was going to bomb the gaming centre, and parents came up to Teju, gave her stern, suspicious looks, and dragged their kids away. The gaming manager was there in a moment, his fingers stuffed into his ears.

'What are you DOING? You cannot upset my

machine this way! I will lose my contract with the mall if the machines wail like this.'

'But I won,' Teju said calmly. There was a short silence as the Manager unplugged the sick and sad machine. 'Fair enough,' he admitted. 'Choose your prize from all those at the counter. Take anything you want. We've never had such a good player here before, so pick the best and biggest prize. But after that, LEAVE!'

Mooshaka-Teju sauntered over to the prize counter and picked the biggest thing there was. It was a red and pink teddy bear, about four feet tall. 'For my dear friend, Orange,' Mooshaka said to himself. 'To play with, when nobody is about!'

* * *

Meanwhile Orange, who was giving himself a ghee-massage on the legs with his trunk, sighed. It had been four hours since he had seen his best friend and he sure missed him. 'Do you want to come back now, Moo?' Orange asked Mooshaka. He spoke in his mind, of course. Mooshaka heard it, of course.

The divine rat understood Orange's loneliness. Besides, the Mall was becoming more crowded and noisy by the minute and Mooshaka's head was beginning to spin with the bright lights and children running this way and that. The adults were no better, constantly screaming and chasing after food and things and their kids. They bumped Mooshaka with their elbows and big shopping bags. He was used to a bit more respect and reverence and thought longingly of the quiet at the temple, which would certainly be closed at this hour for the god's and the priests' afternoon nap.

'Yes,' Mooshaka whispered. 'I want to return home.'

The next instant Mooshaka reappeared in the silver rat statue within the temple. Frozen in his old pose, Mooshaka showed his surprise at being back so suddenly, only with the slightest twitch of his whiskers.

Orange raised a soothing eyebrow at him. 'Every Sunday,' he promised his faithful rat with that one gesture, 'I will send you Into Orbit. You can go in the disguise you choose and spend two hours eating what you will.' Mooshaka flashed him a happy little grin. Then he pushed his silver tongue out a bit at a time, so no human would notice, and calmly licked off the bits of cheese that were still stuck to his whiskers.

The next Sunday and for every Sunday ever after, Mooshaka returned to the mall for his rendezvous with cheese. He went in the form of a small rat, no aunties attached. This was so he could explore the delights of the mall's kitchens in peace. Soon he was sampling cake, cotton candy, hot dogs, idli, samosa, kachori, Chinese fried noodles and all manner of eatables. But his favourite food of all time remained the double cheese pizza.

Occasionally, he transformed himself into a kid in the video game section so he could stun everybody with his speed and skill. The priests at the temple often wondered where all the stuffed toys were coming from, but Orange absolutely loved them. He used them as pillows and foot-rests and belly-rests. If he was in a rough mood, he sometimes punched the toys or kicked them like footballs. Often he tickled Mooshaka's tiny ears and paws with the smaller furry toys, to make him laugh.

On Sunday evenings, both Orange and Mooshaka would contentedly burp their way up to Mount Kailash. In silence, because as Mooshaka reminded the garrulous Orange, on Sunday, even god rests.

THE FUGITIVE FRIEND

Sampurna Chattarji

'So how's the funny bone,' said the doc to the
    writer.
'Don't joke, doc,' said the writer with a long face.
'It's gone! AWOL. Can't find the little blighter.
Ever since I promised those blokes a story, poof!
It upped and left me in the lurch, out of the race,
Down in the dumps, and feeling like the roof
Flew off in a sudden typhoon.
Which is why I'm here, doc, to see if you can help
Get it back, intact, in time, not a second too soon.
My brain feels wet and cloaked in kelp
At the thought that I-me-mine may miss
This chance to do what I do best—
Get the laughs, steal the show, and kiss

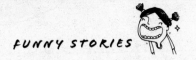

Misfortune goodbye. Oh please, do arrest
The galloping sound of my imminent doom.
Without my funny bone, I'm nothing, doc,
Can't you sense it filling the room—
The reek of sorrow, the taste of rock,
The shooting pains that ring like bells,
The flub of failure, the tick of tock?'
'Calm down, you're overworked, what else,
You need to ease off, and find a way
To recover your funny bone by and by.
Now off you go and have a good day.'

The poor poor writer, dismissed thus,
Without a pill, a potion, or even a hug,
Without the slightest bit of a fuss,
Sent out like a troublesome child
Who hasn't even caught a simple bug!
The writer felt irate and wild.
'Pah! They're fraudsters all, quacks and bums,
Couldn't even tell me where my funny bone's
Gone, leaving me all knees and thumbs.
I think I'll have some jam and scones.
No, too old-fashioned, I'll have a quart
Of the best cold milk with the creamiest tones
To soothe both my stomach and heart.
At the bottom of the glass, perhaps I'll see

My ulnar-ally, my beauteous friend,
Who had the gall to desert poor old me!'
And just as the writer turned the bend
There she was, Kavi, his painter chum.
'Oh hello,' she said, 'Isn't it brill, this lovely light
Full of ochre and tang! No? What's up? Why so
    glum?'

'My funny bone's gone, left me high and dry.
Without it how on earth shall I write
A story that'll make you laugh till you cry?'
'Do I want to?' 'Want to what?' 'Laugh
Till I cry? I've had it with that kind of fun,
Honestly, that silly stuff makes me barf!
Give me, any day, a good old girl on the run
From a family of goons, with her heart on
Her sleeve, and stars in her eyes! Oh sorry,
You're crying, here, have a bon-bon,
And let's sit a bit, there, hail that lorry!
Up you get! Now sit on this sack of what
Is it, beans? How comfy! Now tell me,
Think back, recall, where was the spot
Where you had it last? Can't you see
The light at the end of the tunnel?
We'll find it, I swear, if it takes a year
And a half, from here to the Chunnel

And back to the boonies, I'm by your side,
Look, there's a dhaba, let's grab a bite.
Driver! Stop! And thanks for the ride!
Isn't this the most heartening sight—
All those tables and chairs and glasses
Of tea, and freshly-made rotis with ghee!
Waiter! Get us loads, get us masses
Of all your good stuff, don't you see
My pal's in despair, and it's up to us
To help him find his fugitive friend
Who may have taken the midnight bus
From here to the whole world's end.'

The writer, meanwhile, hadn't said a word.
How could he, with her nonstop chatter!
And so he gloomily ate up the curd
Set before him, and in the midst of the clatter
Looked around him, and almost choked—
'Kavi! Let's ask him!' 'Who, the waiter?'
'No, the cop!' 'What, and get ourselves soaked
In the spit of his scorn, his tears alligator?
No, let's ask the drivers of buses and cabs,
Of lorries and autos and tempos and ricks,
If they've seen your funny bone picking up tabs,
Drawing attention, getting up to his tricks.'

So she, with the writer, went from table to table
Saying, 'Sir, have you seen a funny bone?
That high, that long, the colour of sable?
Call us? Let us know? Here, take my phone
Number, and believe me, it's a matter of life
And of death. You'll be rewarded in stories
Written just for you, your kids and your wife,
Ten times better than momentary glories.'

They were met with laughs, with vacant looks.
Some were stunned and some confused,
Some wanted to flee, thinking they were crooks.
Some listened kindly, patiently bemused.
Some shouted at them for interrupting their meal,
Some said they were mad and needed treatment,
Some offered numbers of herbalists who heal
Every single kind of mysterious ailment.

Exhausted, insulted, tired and sad,
They came at last to the end of their tether
Where sat an unassuming young lad
Who looked as if whatever the weather
He'd be fine, he'd stay fit, he'd never be ill,
Never down with measles, dengue or mumps.
The kind who always offers to pay the bill,
And never has anything to do with chumps.

'What's the prob?' he asked, pulling out two chairs.
'Can I help? Tell me all! Ah, I see, oh my god,
I can tell that you're caught in the cross-hairs
Of a terrible loss. Listen, it may seem odd,
But here's the thing, you're getting it wrong.
Your funny bone, your essential *humerus*
Hasn't scooted or sold himself for a song.
What he's done is in response to the numerous
Times you've misused him—he's settling a score.
He's not lost at all, just dislocated! Haven't you
Felt that tingling jolt, that strange sickening sore
When a thing's out of joint, all bruised and blue,
That feeling of "oh no, I'm not myself today,
Who am I, why do I live?" Yes, I feel your pain,
And no, it's not here to stay.
Hold out your arm, now look at that stain
On the wall and pretend I'm not here—
Oops! Sorry, that hurt just a bit, but guess what,
He's back and won't run away, have no fear,
If you promise him a sweet little perk on the spot.
Twenty per cent of your fee and a share of the
      fame
That you rightfully owe to your writerly mate,
Fair is fair and it's all in the game.
Gotta go now, goodbye, I'm getting quite late!'

And off he shot, like a runner from the block,
Leaving writer and painter all numb
From the joy and the pain and the shock.
Had even garrulous Kavi gone dumb?
No! No such luck. 'Hip-hip and hooray,
And jingle bells too, how's it feel to be back,
Reunited with buddy and ready to play?'
'Oh no!' said the writer. 'Alas and alack!
What have I done? Now I have no excuse
To put off the writing, I have no way out!
What shall I say, now I've lost my last ruse?
It's all your fault, Kavi, for being so eager,
Why didn't you just throw up your hands
Instead of rushing to help like a beaver!
Now I'm stuck, ooh, help! My thyroid glands
Are swelling like balloons, and my liver
Is spotting, my pancreas bust.
I'm weak, I'm aching, I'm all a-shiver.
It's the viral, it's the flu, bird or swine,
I'm burning with fever,
And tied up with twine.
My eyes feel like corkscrews,
My throat is all jagged,
My innards have come loose,
My nails are all ragged.
My spleen has stopped fighting.

FUNNY STORIES

My thigh has a cramp, my mind is a whirl.
How will I ever get back to writing?
My fingers shake, my nerves are on edge.
My jaw is locked, and I need a new hip.
I'm nauseous and giddy like I've swallowed a
    hedge.
Ouch! And I've only this minute dislocated my lip.'

This poem is dedicated to Tina

RAMA AIMS ...

Adithi Rao

Putta's best friend was Rama. He had other friends, of course, but Rama was the best-est of them all. In fact, Putta and Rama were so thick that they were what kids today would call BFFs.

Only, Putta was born in the 1950s, when terms like BFF (Best Friends Forever) hadn't come into vogue yet. In the town of Mysore in Karnataka, friends addressed each other as "malla", "koti maga" or "maharaya". The first meant "duffer", the second meant "son of a monkey" and the third meant "great king".

Putta called Rama "maharaya". Rama's father was a gentleman named Dasharath, and hailed from a place called Ayodhya. Rama was pretty handy with a bow, and Dasharath was a famous politician in those parts, so the term "maharaya" was really quite appropriate. Rama enjoyed the easy banter he exchanged with his young friend. He had a special place for Putta in his heart, and was always happy to bail him out of trouble any time the boy called for help.

All Putta had to do was go into a dark room, close his eyes and mumble, 'Maharaya?' and lo! Rama would appear, complete with bow and arrow, smiling all over his handsome blue face. Then Putta was free to place his request.

This time the request went like this: 'Maharaya, the Maths homework is due first thing in the morning, and that useless Rajagopal Sir has set us so many sums to do that no mortal boy would be able to complete it in just one night. Not without sitting down for a full half hour that is. Please fix the problem for me.'

Of course, sitting for half an hour over maths sums was not an option. And why should it be? Which ten-year-old friend of Rama ever needed to waste time over such mundane matters? Besides, the problem wasn't so simple. That wily old Rajagopal was a regular customer at Ganesh Dosa House ...

Ganesh Dosa House was a splendid little restaurant with wooden benches, situated in the very heart of Mysore. Appaji Rao, Putta's father, was the proprietor of the establishment. Dosas and idlis were served piping hot and dripping with freshly churned butter. The restaurant also served the finest coffee. It was no wonder that Rajagopal and Krishna Shastri (Putta's Mathematics teacher and school Principal, respectively), would be standing outside the wooden doors of the restaurant at 6 every morning. The instant the doors were thrown open, the two pedagogues would hitch up their dhotis and charge inside as if competing with hordes of hungry townspeople. (In fact, they were Appaji Rao's only customers at that time of the day.)

They would unerringly head for their customary bench in the centre of the room. Within five minutes Choodamani the waiter, without being asked to, would place a plate of steaming hot idlis before Krishna Shastri, and a crisp butter dosa before Rajagopal. This is what happened every morning, with unfailing regularity. The moment the last bite of dosa had been ingested and the last piece of idli burped up, steaming cups of coffee would arrive. Then the bill would be paid, and after that the two men would ... *not* leave.

And that was the bad part for Putta. Because, in addition to the bill of four rupees twenty-five paise, the teachers paid Appaji Rao for his hospitality by sharing every misadventure (imagined and otherwise) of his eldest son-and heir in school the previous day. They would talk, enact, and gesticulate. On one occasion, they even sang to enhance the performance!

Appaji Rao would listen intently, frequently shuddering with horror. When the teachers were certain that they had sealed their naughty pupil's fate, they considered their business at Ganesh Dosa House complete for the day. With one final belch in parting tribute to the cook Bangara, they would unhitch their dhotis and trudge off to school in time to ring the morning bell.

Appaji Rao would then cross the fence that separated the restaurant from his house and yell for his son. Putta would present himself in uniform, try to look unconcerned and fail miserably. Appaji Rao would proceed to berate the boy at the top of his voice in the most colourful language (which his other three sons would hide behind the kitchen door and hurriedly commit to memory).

Then he would drive home the message with a sound thrashing, and pack Putta off to school.

And this is how Putta's day began. Everyday.

And this is why Putta was on his knees that night, yelling for Rama.

I'm sure that an adult reading this would shake his head in disapproval. But all my young friends will understand Putta's predicament, and extend their sympathies from the bottom of their ... bottoms.

Rama, obliging as always, arrived within seconds of being summoned.

'There you are, maharaya!' cried Putta in joyful relief. 'Won't you please fix this problem for me?' he asked.

Rama merely smiled and withdrew an arrow from his quiver. He secured it in place, drew his bow string and took aim. Then he released the arrow with a loud, resounding twang!

The arrow whizzed past Putta's ear, grazing the tip of it and making him jump. It seems Rama's aim had gone a bit awry! Rubbing his offended organ, Putta looked around quickly. The arrow had vanished. When he turned back to look at the blue-man himself, he was gone too. But Putta felt unconcerned. This is how it always happened

42

(except for that brush with the arrow, of course). And Rama had never failed him yet. So he took a deep, confident breath, lay down on his mat, and went off to sleep a full two hours before the rest of the household.

When Appaji Rao came home and found his eldest snoring under the blankets, he frowned.

'Doesn't this useless chap have any studying to do?' he demanded.

'Leave him. Let him sleep!' cried Lalithamma, the fond mother, rushing to the rescue. 'He is tired, poor child.'

'Poor child, my foot!' snorted Appaji. 'This fellow is only fit to become a waiter in my restaurant. Better stop his schooling now and save money on the fees ...'

Appaji Rao went off grumbling to wash up for dinner. Lalithamma, after adjusting the blanket over Putta, returned to the kitchen. Her husband's threats caused no sense of foreboding in her. She knew he didn't mean a word of it.

The next morning, Putta plastered down his unruly curls with water, ate his butter dosa and went off to school. The Maths homework was in his satchel untouched, the space under each question blank. Putta whistled a little tune under his breath as he walked, his three younger brothers sleepily trudging after him in single file. They were holding on to each other, and Murali, the first in queue, had grabbed on to the straps of Putta's school bag for support. Gradually Putta started to feel the weight of them dragging him backwards. He turned around and saw that all three had their eyes closed. They were practically sleepwalking, and he was lugging everyone's weight!

'Idiots! I'll teach them a lesson!' he thought. He struggled on until they reached the pond. Instead of walking past, he dashed straight at it, stepping aside smartly at the last second so that the three walked right into the water fully-clothed! Splash! Putta ran away, leaving them sputtering in indignation, soaked to the bone.

'They won't try that again in a hurry,' he chuckled, as he entered the school gates.

It was well into the second period when he glanced outside the classroom window and caught sight of his mother leading his siblings across the school courtyard, where the national flag fluttered gently on the pole. They must have gone home howling to be changed into fresh, dry uniforms by their sympathetic mother. She had accompanied them back to school to request Krishna Shastri to excuse them for their tardiness. She caught Putta's laughing eyes through the grill of the Class 5 classroom window and shook her fist angrily at him. Putta grinned back cheekily. He knew she would never tell on him to the Principal, and she'd roast her other three sons alive if they tried to do so. Putta was her pet. She would never let him down.

Besides, Rama had shot his arrow (albeit a little off centre), and once that happened, nothing ever went wrong in the day. Putta had been bailed out of trouble too many times by Rama's benevolent arrows to have even a moment's doubt ...

'Putta!' Rajagopal's voice cracked through his reverie, making him jump. 'Bring me your Mathematics notebook!'

Putta smiled a secret smile. The last time he had failed to do his homework, Rajagopal had summoned him with these very words. Putta had taken his book to the teacher, opened at the tell-tale page. Then, just as Rajagopal had been about to glance down at it, the school peon Susainathan had arrived to announce that the Principal wanted to see Rajagopal urgently.

The Maths teacher had hurried away, forgetting all about Putta's homework. There, for some inexplicable reason, he had got into an argument with the Principal, and the two had actually come to blows. Rajagopal, a full head shorter than his colleague, had come off the worse, and had to be taken to the local dispensary to have his cuts bound up.

Of course, Krishna Shastri never did understand what happened that day. All he knew was that within seconds of Rajagopal's departure for the doctor's, he was suddenly filled with the deepest remorse for beating up his friend. He had visited Rajagopal at his residence later that day armed with a box of laddoos, and peace had been reestablished. The next morning it was business as usual, and the two had been sighted breakfasting at the Ganesh Dosa House.

'I wonder who will beat up whom this time,' smirked Putta, as he laid his untouched homework down on the table before Rajagopal. 'Maybe Srini and I can get the others to lay a wager on Rajagopal's chances against Krishna Shastri!'

'Dream out of the window, will you?'

demanded Rajagopal. Putta met his eyes confidently and said nothing. The teacher lowered his head and his gaze fell on the blank answer spaces.

'Wait!' Putta's brain screamed. 'He's not supposed to see that!'

At that precise moment, there was a sound from the door, and Putta automatically spun around. Susainathan had arrived! Rama to the rescue!

'Sir, Boss wanting see you. This boy also. This boy ...' he announced in broken English, gesturing towards Putta.

Both pupil and teacher frowned. They looked at each other. Rajagopal blinked. Then he left the classroom without a word, and Putta followed.

They entered the Principal's office. Putta's mother was there, looking at him accusingly. What followed was like a well-rehearsed nightmare. Shastri caught up his cane and whacked Putta soundly for "drowning" his siblings. When he had finished, Lalithamma—that gentle soul— stepped forward and slapped her pride-and-joy about the head. Then, so as not to be outdone by the other two, Rajagopal grabbed the cane

out of Krishna Shastri's hand and paddled Putta
for failing to do his homework.

Putta's brain had frozen in shock.

None of those beatings—nor the one he
received from Appaji later that day—hurt as much
as Rama's betrayal ...

Putta didn't touch his dinner that night. He
saw remorse on his mother's face as she hovered
around him anxiously with the serving spoon in
her hand. He did not mean to torment her. He
knew it was not her fault that the day had turned
into such a disaster. It was Rama's. He had lost
his Rama. His BFF. His maharaya. He did not even
call for Rama because he wouldn't have known
what to say if they were face to face. He felt
dazed and bereft.

But as Putta lay down on his mat that
night and silent tears rolled down his cheeks
in the darkness, the room was suddenly lit up
by a strange blue light. He frowned and raised
his head.

Rama!

Rama seemed blurred. No wait, that was
because Putta was looking at him through the
tears. But then Putta too seemed hazy to Rama,
because Rama too was crying!

In the momentary silence, Putta blinked and his vision cleared. The arrows in Rama's quiver seemed to have wilted, and his bow looked so forlorn! When he saw his best friend weeping, Putta's anger vanished.

He jumped up and ran to his friend. 'What is it? What happened?'

Rama only shook his head. Putta took his arm and led him to the wooden stool in the corner of the room.

'Maharaya,' he urged, 'talk to me! Maybe I can help?'

Rama gave a hiccup. 'T ... there isn't ... anything ... y ... you or any ... one can do. I've lost my d ... direction, that's all!' he finished, before breaking into sobs again.

Putta frowned, regarding his friend in puzzlement. Whatever did he mean? Suddenly he remembered the wayward arrow from the previous night, and his fingers automatically went to his ear. Was that misdirected arrow the reason behind everything going wrong that day?

And if it was, why should it be so? Rama's focus could never have gone amiss. Only his aim. It seemed to have been just a little off to one side. And yet, wasn't it possible that a tiny error like that could have big, big repercussions in Ayodhya, Rama's headquarters?

Suddenly the solution hit Putta right between the eyes, almost like one of those arrows Rama had once been so good at shooting! He jumped up and grabbed Rama's arms.

'Maharaya, blink! Blink, I tell you, quickly! Get all those tears out of your eyes and look at me! Hurry!'

Rama was bemused, but did as he was told, because the boy seemed so insistent. Putta, meanwhile, had hurried away to the far corner of the room and was holding up something – Rama couldn't see what exactly.

'How much is this?' cried Putta.

'How much is what?' asked Rama, squinting slightly to get a better look.

'This! These fingers that I'm holding up. How many?'

'Er ... two. Three. No, two. *Definitely* two. I think. Or maybe three? Er ...'

Putta clapped his hands and burst out laughing. So *that* was the problem. How simple!

'Look, can you meet me at the Good Eyes Opticians down by the City Bus Stand tomorrow afternoon? I'll come there directly from school.

Oh, and in the meanwhile, could you find something else to wear?'

'Why,' asked Rama puzzled, glancing down at his blue chest with its many gold ornaments, and his beautiful cream silk dhoti. 'What's wrong with what I'm wearing now?'

'Nothing!' Putta reassured him hurriedly. 'It is quite gorgeous, really. Just pull on a shirt over your dhoti. And less gold chains. Or better still, no gold chains.'

'Why?'

'Er ... someone might steal them.'

'Oh. Well, okay then, I'll leave them with my Sita. She's Goddess Lakshmi incarnate, anyway. She'll take care of them for me till I get back.'

The next afternoon at 4, Putta found a blueish coloured man standing outside the Good Eyes Opticians by the bus stand, sporting a polka-dotted bright pink shirt over his silk dhoti. Putta nearly had a heart attack! But when Rama spotted him, he beamed so proudly that Putta didn't have the heart to prick his bubble.

'How do I look?' asked Rama.

'Like a picture!' exclaimed Putta. He didn't say a picture of what.

'Hanuman picked it for me,' beamed Rama.

Putta's eyes softened. 'Ah,' he thought, 'My maharaya's other BFF.' He gave Rama a thumbs-up sign and led him inside the spectacle shop.

Half an hour later they came out. This time Rama was wearing a pair of glasses on his nose.

'Think Sita will like it?' he asked, patting the frames.

'She'll love it! Now come on. People are staring,' mumbled Putta, hurrying his friend away.

'Don't take this personally, but I think it's your school uniform. That blue-and-white combination is not right. Blue should be the colour of your *skin*, not your clothes. That's why people are staring.'

'Yes,' sighed Putta resignedly. 'That's probably it.'

Rama's aim never went off the mark again. He used his arrows well from that day onwards. And because of this, Putta is now a middle-aged multi-millionaire owner of a chain of five-star hotels called the Ganesh Luxury Resorts. Ravana (and not Vibhishana) is dead. And thanks to those well-aimed arrows, Sita is back from Lanka and safe in Ayodhya where she belongs.

The reason you never see a statue of Lord Rama with spectacles on his nose is because he has moved with the times and switched to contact lenses!

PLAY DATE FROM HELL

Nalini Sorensen

'**A**wesome!' Ari yelled out, right into his mum's face. 'I've been waiting to go to his house for SO long now ...'

'Calm down, it's just a play date, Aryan,' his mum answered, replying to the text, and then plugging her mobile back into the charger on the table.

Ari rolled his eyes. But only when his mum wasn't looking. She was getting tough on him these days. She kept saying these pre-tween years were essential in setting boundaries and guidelines. And scarily enough, now more than ever, she seemed to have eyes at the back of her head.

'Don't roll your eyes, Ari,' she said, without turning around, giving him a start.

'How do you even do that?' he asked.

'A-ha! I know stuff,' his mum replied. He could hear the victory in her voice.

He laughed. 'You've replied yes, right?' he asked, and then ran off to his room, after she nodded. He was just dying to go to Ben's house. Ben was the new boy in school. He had recently moved to Mumbai. His mum was Indian and his dad was American. He looked Indian, but he had a strong American accent. Just like the kids in the movies. Friday couldn't come fast enough.

* * *

On Friday, Ben's mum picked them up from school. She dropped them to his building and went off on some work. Ari and Ben rode the elevator up to his flat, with the watchman. This had never happened to Ari before in his eleven-year-old life. He was an only child and his mum was a little over protective. His eyes shone with excitement. He was lapping up the freedom and independence.

Inside the elevator, Ari saw a picture of a missing dog, stuck on the mirror.

'Sad, huh?' Ari said, pointing to it.

'It is. Very. It's like our dog, you know?' said Ben.

'Oh. Oh no! I had no idea,' Ari replied, just as the elevator door opened. 'What happened? How did ... Buddy go missing?'

'We don't exactly know,' Ben mumbled. 'The door was like open and then ...'

He was interrupted as the elevator stopped, and the doors flew open. The two of them rang the doorbell, and as the front door opened, there were two dogs that threw themselves on Ben and Ari. Ben shook his bag off his shoulder and lay down, flat on the ground, and let the dogs freely lick him all over. Ari knew he was not supposed to stare, but the entire scene looked just so delightful. It was full of dog tails wagging and licks and woofs and laughter.

'Okay then, down boy. Down, Max,' Ben said, patting the bigger of the two dogs.

'You too, Rene,' he added.

The dogs paid absolutely no attention. They continued to run around and lick and jump on the two boys, in sheer delight. Ari could feel his face wet with dog saliva. He could feel some fur tickling his nose.

Ari peeked inside the flat some more and saw two cats, lying in the sunshine, near the big window in the living room, giving him and Ben utterly disgusted looks. And up in the corner, below a big painting of a sunset, was a fish tank.

'Oh my God, Dude! How many pets do you have here?'

'Well, the three dogs … Well, like two now. Ya know, about Buddy. Then two cats and some fish,' Ben replied. 'That used to be like quite normal in the US.'

'Dude! That's really not normal here. I have nothing,' Ari replied, utterly fascinated.

'Yah, it's because we lived in a house in the US. Here, in an apartment, space is like a problem, you know? You wanna go to my room?'

'Sure,' Ari said, just as the doorbell rang again.

In walked Ben's twin younger brothers. In just a matter of seconds, before they could even put their bags down, they got into a fight and started pushing and shoving each other and ended up wrestling on the floor; punches flying wildly.

'Oooof!' said one voice.

'I'll get you back,' said another muffled voice.

'Break it up! Break it up!' came a third voice. This one was Ben's household helper. She separated the twins, and stared them down. Then she looked at Ari and Ben, and asked, 'Boys, do you want to eat something? Are you hungry?'

That caught the attention of all four boys. Ari and Ben nodded. The twins nodded.

'Okay,' she continued, 'Ben, you and your friend, go to your room. I will bring it there. And Chris and Sammy, you two come with me.'

'Those are your brothers?' Ari whispered to Ben, as they left the living room and headed towards Ben's room.

'Yup. Twins. Cool dudes, really. But, they are like the little brothers from hell. This was them behaving well,' Ben replied.

'I didn't even know you had brothers! Which school do they go to?'

'Oh, I don't know the name. It's a school near home. Like, just down the street, actually. They didn't have space for them in our school, as the school does not put twins in the same class. They have to be in like different classes, and one class was full. My mom says, the school says they should get admission in our school like next year,' said Ben.

They walked into Ben's room and Ari stopped.

It was the most awesome room he had ever laid his eyes on. There were clothes on the floor, random Lego pieces, and fully assembled Lego masterpieces everywhere, a tiny TV in the corner, connected to an Xbox, and toys absolutely everywhere – remote controlled cars, swords, soccer balls, tennis racquets, Pokemon cards … It was every boy's dream come true.

'Dude! Your room is awesome!'

'Yeah, my mom is not allowed to come in here. Our helper like comes in to do the floors, but she's not allowed to touch anything,' said Ben.

'And your mum allows this?' Ari asked, completely baffled.

'Dude, did you not just meet my twin brothers? I'm like the good one around here. I pretty much get my way on most things, as they have to like cope with the crazy, uncontrollable twins,' he laughed.

Ari couldn't reply. He just threw his head back and laughed along with Ben.

Meena, the household helper, came in with a tray of sandwiches, popcorn and chocolate milk. She set it down on a table in the corner of his room.

'What's your name?' she asked.

'Aryan, but everyone calls me Ari,' Ari replied.

'Ah. You and Ben are good friends?'

'Yes. I mean he's new. But yah, we are good friends,' Ari said.

She nodded and then gestured to sit on the chair and eat.

They could hear thuds and bumps from outside Ben's room and it was clear Chris and Sammy were at it again. Meena sighed loudly and said, 'I will be back. Eat properly, okay?'

She left the room calmly enough, but started yelling, 'Break it up! Break it up!' as soon as she was out.

The boys sat down and polished off the food quickly.

'Do you want to like play on the Xbox?' Ben asked.

'Sure,' Ari replied. 'Which one do you want to play?'

'I was thinking like FIFA.'

'Awesome! I don't have the latest one. I can see you do.'

They were standing in front of the TV, totally engrossed with what was on the screen, when suddenly one of the cats leaped into Ben's room. Max and Rene followed at top speed. It was like a blur of fur. The cat jumped onto Ben's bed and the dogs followed, and then it was on the bookshelf, and the next thing Ari saw, as he turned, was books flying everywhere, Lego flying everywhere, and a cat tail flying out of the room.

'SIMBA!' Ben screamed furiously, just as Meena ran into the room.

'What happened here?' Meena asked taking in the damage.

'Max and Rene chasing Simba again,' Ben explained.

'Oh no! Look at this mess!' Meena cried.

'We can help you?' Ari asked.

Meena brought over the instructions for the biggest Lego masterpiece that had got shattered. 'Can you boys make this one again?' she asked.

Ari and Ben sat down to it. They collected all the broken Lego bits and blocks together and started trying to fit it all back in place.

Meanwhile, Meena put the bookshelf back upright and started stacking the books on it. Time seemed to fly by, only interrupted by loud peels of laughter coming in from the living room.

Meena looked up worriedly, as she stacked the last of the books on the shelf. It sounded like Chris and Sammy were having the best time.

Ben too looked up and said to Ari, 'Dude, let's go like see what they are up to.'

All three of them walked into the living room. There they saw Chris and Sammy sliding all over the floor. It looked extremely slippery and the boys were slipping and sliding all over the place. They looked like they were skating barefoot all over the floor.

'What have you done? Chris? Sammy? What have you put on the floor?' Meena asked shrilly.

'It's the powder for the carrom board!' Chris screeched.

'It makes the floor so slippery. Look! Weeeeeeee!' Sammy added, sliding all the way to where they were standing.

'Dude, let's like try this!' Ben yelled.

Ari didn't need to be told twice. The four of them were slipping and sliding all over the place, when the doorbell rang.

It was Ari's mum to pick him up. She saw the floor white with powder and the boys sliding about. She saw Simba jump up on the dining table and Max and Rene try to jump after her, and then slide and yelp loudly. She saw Meena looking apologetically at her. She stared at the entire scene, in shocked silence.

'Errm. I think I saw the missing dog from the elevator poster, downstairs in the lobby,' Ari's mum said to Meena.

'Sorry, Madam? What was that?' Meena asked, as the doorbell rang again.

Ari's mum was right! It was the watchman with the missing Buddy!

'Buddy! Where were ya? Come here, boy!' Ben screamed with joy and all three siblings slid over to Buddy. They were a huge bundle of boys and fur and tails rolling about on the slippery floor of the living room. Rene and Max were right in the mix too. Simba however, stayed put on the table.

Ari's mum managed to extract him from all of this, and shut the door.

They got into the elevator and you could hear the air move in the sheer silence. As the lift went down another floor, his mum said in an icy cold voice, 'Well, that seemed like a play date from hell.'

'Not really,' Ari replied. 'Can we have another tomorrow?'

OF PLANTS, COFFEE AND KIDS

Devika Rangachari

Having spent most of my schooldays in a gentle, book-induced trance, it was obvious to everyone that I would either vanish into the pages of a book or write one myself. The latter happened to everyone's evident relief and delight, and so, I now spend my days scribbling away or with my head in the pages of my latest manuscript. However, being an author does not simply mean that I churn out stories at my desk day-after-day, perhaps nibbling on some chocolate and occasionally staring out of the window to seek inspiration. No, a writer's life isn't that easy! For being one also means that I sometimes have to change out of my comfortable home clothes and dress smartly so that I can visit schools and brave the eyes and questions of hundreds of curious children and staff members while I talk about my work.

On one occasion, I drive up to the gates of a school in a cloud of dust. This is because the taxi driver is somewhat theatrical and likes to do things with a flourish. He speeds up dramatically as we approach along the potholed road, one hand on the pressure horn. And so the world at large is alerted to my arrival. I blink the grit from my eyes, wait for the dust to settle and then approach the irritable guards. I am immediately embroiled in an argument.

'Why are you here?' they demand, eyeing me and my bag of books with deep suspicion. To them, I am someone with a nefarious purpose, likely to be up to no good the minute they let me in.

'The school has invited me,' I bleat, cowed into instant submission by their fierce moustaches.

'Who has invited you?'

'The school!' I realise, belatedly, that I do not know the name of the librarian, which could have been the password in question.

'Where have you come from?' they persist.

'From Delhi. The school's also in Delhi,' I add brightly.

They go back and forth, debating geographical contours, the probability or otherwise of my having been extended an invitation by the school, the possibly explosive contents of my bag and so on. They have not, however, bargained for one simple fact – an author is usually good with words.

And so, I eventually win the battle and rush in before they change their minds and haul me back.

I am taken to the principal's room but I am clearly not worthy of entering the hallowed premises.

'Wait here,' the escort teacher tells me, waving me to a long bench by the door. 'The principal is *very* busy.' Her tone is accusatory. The underlying message is clear: it is people like me who commit the unforgivable crime of wasting others' time. Therefore, it is fitting that I am to sit on a bench meant for offenders. I soon discover that I am sharing it with a small boy with a mutinous expression, who is waiting to be hauled in and punished. As time wears on and there is no sign of anyone, I begin to feel as guilty as him and we squirm in unison. I am wondering whether to make a hasty exit and am mentally measuring the distance to the gate when the Hallowed One is suddenly before me.

'What is your opinion of Janmashtami?' she asks, sternly.

I rise to my feet and gape at her. 'I ... well ...' I begin when the Hallowed One cuts me short and hails a distant teacher.

'What is your opinion of Janmashtami?' she bellows across the corridor.

The beleaguered teacher stammers in confusion. 'It ... it is important. It should ...'

The Hallowed One raises a hand majestically, and then turns and walks off. As I have no further instructions, I decide to follow her. We proceed down a series of corridors until she hands me over to a teacher and vanishes.

'You will be interacting with Class 7,' the teacher says.

We turn the corner and come upon an open space – a sort of courtyard that connects the corridors and faces a block of classrooms. It is noisy and the decibel levels rise as the rows of students sitting in the middle of the courtyard see me. This is where I am to have my session.

'Oh, this is Class 8!' the teacher exclaims. She does not seem too bothered, though, to figure out where the original class has been spirited away.

I wait patiently as the teachers try and restore order. The children's shrieks combine with the chatter of a horde of students who are lounging around in the corridors and the courtyard, and with the dull roars and thumps emanating from the classrooms around. And all the while, I am being scrutinised by bright-yet-puzzled eyes. Perhaps everyone is wondering why and how I managed to infiltrate their school.

'Start!' A teacher suddenly presses a microphone into my hands.

I start to speak when I see a couple of hundred children making their way towards us.

'Don't start until everyone's here,' the teacher admonishes me. The unfairness of this takes my breath away. I am struggling to think of a suitable retort when I realise there are even more children coming from another direction.

'I didn't want more than 150 students,' I begin firmly. 'There are over 500 here. I ...'

The teacher cuts me short. 'Please wait till everyone is seated. No one can hear you.'

Then she turns to the children. 'See, this is an author,' she announces with the air of one embarking on a scientific experiment.

All eyes are on me now, most of them coldly appraising. So *this* is an author, I can hear them think. Short and thin with wild hair. They are clearly not impressed.

Every beginning has an end. Clinging to this thought, I start the session, counting the moments until my deliverance. I talk for a while about books and reading.

'... and so this is why being an author is fun,' I conclude, at long last. 'Any questions?'

I am immediately besieged by what seems like a million queries delivered by voice tones ranging from the polite to the outright querulous.

'Did you read all day at school?'

'Are books really that important?'

'Did you read *and* do your homework?'

'I love books but my mother says that reading doesn't help and ...'

'Why can't school be all about stories?'

'Did you ever meet a famous author?'

'Are *you* a famous author?'

'I love to write stories but my mother says it doesn't help and ...'

I am right in the middle of answering their questions when a teacher suddenly raises her hand. 'Will you please talk to them about books and reading?' she asks plaintively. 'This is why they are here, after all.'

I stare at her, mystified, when a hush suddenly descends on the crowd. Everyone is looking at a point behind me, so I turn. I can't see anything or anyone, so I turn back. The silence continues, so I look behind me again – just in time to see the Hallowed One peeping out from behind a pillar. This is, perhaps, her idea of fun.

'Continue,' she says grandly, waving a hand in my direction. She has now emerged fully from hiding.

I turn to the audience and continue for a couple of minutes when a hand falls on my arm. It belongs to one of the teachers.

'Principal Ma'am wants to give you a plant,' she says in tones of mingled reverence and envy.

I am about to be irrevocably blessed. Oh, joy! A gift from the Hallowed One, no less!

So they stop, mid-flow, and the plant-presentation happens.

'Now please wrap up everything in five minutes,' the teacher hisses at me. 'These are very busy children.'

The minute I stop, the Hallowed One approaches the group of teachers. 'What is your opinion of Janmashtami?' she asks them.

I race out of the school, clutching the plant, past the bemused guards and into the safety of my car. I vow not to subject myself to this again.

* * *

For some days, I lurk in the comfortable confines of my room, my head swarming with ideas and stories and other pleasant thoughts when the dreaded summons arrives again. I am to visit yet another school to talk about my work. Pushing away thoughts of my earlier experience, I embark on this mission, pale but determined.

This time, I have to get to a school on the outskirts of the city, located within the premises of a gated community and named after it. I am armed with a map and a series of instructions. Getting to the school is a nightmare, though – a combination of my terrible sense of direction and the taxi driver's ego that does not permit him to ask for help. Consequently, we wander round and round in widening circles until, quite fortuitously, we stumble upon the correct gate.

Once in, the receptionist refuses to acknowledge that I have a pre-arranged session with the students of Class 7.

'The librarian is in the hospital,' she tells me accusingly, as though I have helped put her there.

No amount of arguing and glaring and appointment-checking can budge her from her stance.

Eventually, another teacher strides up and asks what the problem is. She then offers a truly brilliant solution. 'We have eight sections in Class 7,' she says. 'So we'll take you to each of them and you can conduct your sessions.'

More arguing and glaring – to no avail.

'I will not conduct eight sessions in your school,' I declare firmly. 'That is simply too much!'

This is followed by yet more arguing and glaring!

It takes them ages to hammer out a compromise formula. Fifty 'select' students will sit in on the session. 'And you will have to settle for that,' the teacher snarls. 'We can't give you any more.'

I begin to tell her that I don't *want* any more but then subside into silence. This is a losing battle.

'Will you have coffee?' the receptionist chips in.

I turn to her gratefully. 'I don't drink coffee. Could I have some tea instead?'

'Sure,' she says and, a minute later, hands me a mug brimming with milky coffee.

It is too late to wonder whether this is sheer cussedness or stupidity on her part because I am now being ushered away by a third person who calls herself the librarian.

'But aren't you supposed to be in hospital?' I ask, mystified.

'Not now,' she replies. (Not *now*? Do the librarians of this school take turns to visit the hospital?) 'I am here,' she adds, somewhat unnecessarily. 'It is the other.'

I don't bother to ask what this impossibly vague statement means and trail behind her obediently. The librarian takes me to a cavernous library and motions to a footstool.

'Sit here,' she says sternly as if she suspects I will turn cartwheels or dance on it instead. Thereafter, she proceeds to lecture me on her problems with the school management and how it would serve them right if I didn't do the session after all and just billed them for the transport and so on. Our thrilling talk is interrupted by the fifty 'select' children who solemnly file into a room off the library. The librarian treats this as a mere annoyance and swings back into her details of subterfuge while I listen, open-mouthed. Meanwhile, I furtively deposit the milky coffee on the desk behind me.

At some point, the librarian stops in the middle of her rant and gestures irritably towards the room.

'Do your session,' she says, 'but no more than forty-five minutes. The children have to be somewhere after that.'

I enter the room with much trepidation but begin to enjoy myself enormously a couple of minutes later. This is the brightest, most delightful bunch I have ever interacted with. Time flies and forty-five minutes later, when I tell them it is time to wind up, there is an immediate uproar.

'Just ten more minutes!' they plead.

And 'Ten more minutes?' they coax, ten minutes later.

I peep into the main library and the Disgruntled One has vanished. 'But you have to be "somewhere",' I tell the kids.

'We don't have to be anywhere,' they assure me. 'This is a free period. So please go on?'

I continue for fifteen minutes and then another twenty. There is no sign of any teacher all this while. I could just as easily have kidnapped the lot, jumped out of the window, bundled them into my car (I would have had to convert it into a stretch limousine, but still ...) and driven them away for some dark, sinister purpose.

An hour later, I give up. 'You *have* to go!' I say sternly. 'Someone will be looking for you.'

'No one is,' they chorus. I pretend not to hear and hustle them into a line.

'Do you know how to get back to your classroom?' I ask anxiously.

'Do *you* know how to get back to the main gate?' they retort.

I don't, so I enlist the services of the nearest boy to escort me. On the way out, he says he's had the most fun ever and could I come every day to chat with them? There is still no sign of any teacher or adult figure to question what these children are doing roaming around the corridors.

I pass the receptionist once again who stares at me blankly before something stirs in her eyes. I beat a hasty retreat to my car as I hear her call out behind me, 'Coffee …?'

THE HAIRCUT

Sowmya Rajendran

Shivani's hair was the joint property of her mother and grandmother. Amma and Ammamma did not agree about most things since they were daughter-in-law – mother-in-law and it would have broken the hearts of saas-bahu serial producers if they'd got along just fine. But Shivani's hair was the one thing they agreed upon.

It had to be long, it had to be strong. But Shivani couldn't shampoo with any of those evil foreign brands that would make her hair fall and leave her bald by age twenty. In which case, nobody would marry her. And so, the senior women of the family strongly believed that Shivani should wash her hair only with homemade shikakai.

A concoction that Ammamma painstakingly prepared from scratch every three months.

'I look like I have dreadlocks!' Shivani wailed, looking at the mirror. The new pimple on her nose glowed like a 100-watt bulb. Darn this muggy Chennai weather, it always turned her face into a road full of potholes and bumps. And she had gained two kilos last month! At fourteen, when most girls were transforming from ugly ducklings to beautiful swans, Shivani seemed to be turning from duckling to duck.

'It's good for your hair,' admonished her mother.

'*How?*' Shivani howled. 'How can this possibly be good?! If anything, it makes my hair dirtier!'

But Amma had already walked out of the room. Clearly, she was not a woman who believed that dialogue could resolve anything. No wonder the world was such a violent place, Shivani grumbled. Most people were like her mother. Unwilling to sit across a table and talk things out.

She ate her idlis in silence, refusing to look up from the plate. Maybe then, her insensitive and intolerant family would notice that *something* was wrong with her. They would realise that Shivani was depressed. They would understand that their extreme neglect of her needs had led to this sad situation. Shivani would be taken to hospital. The psychiatrist would chide her family for being such tyrants. And then, after a month of medication, Shivani would emerge from the hospital looking radiant after a shampoo bath.

'Want a vada?' asked Ammamma.

Shivani's grandmother thought that food could cure anything. Including obesity. Yesterday, when Shivani had burst into tears after the button in her favourite red top popped open because her stomach couldn't fit in there any more, Ammamma had offered to make her badam halwa.

Now, Shivani shook her head resolutely to indicate that her sorrows were beyond the realm of vadas and halwa.

'Just three idlis you are eating?' asked Ammamma, rolling her eyes. 'No wonder you look so weak. When I was your age, boys used to queue up outside my house to get a glimpse of my ample curves.'

Shivani dunked a piece of idli in her sambhar without indicating that she'd heard Ammamma. But Ammamma was not one to be cowed down by such a show of indifference. She even spoke to people on TV in moments when she felt not sharing her wisdom immediately would lead to the end of the world.

'Want some gulab jamun?' Ammamma persisted. 'Good for digestion.'

Shivani got up from the table and marched to the kitchen, plate in hand.

Ammamma was not ruffled in the least. She continued the conversation with the jug of water on the table.

'Have you taken everything?' Amma asked as Shivani strapped her bag on, ready to run downstairs and wait for the school bus.

Shivani didn't bother replying. Yes, she had taken everything. Including the 500 rupees that she'd saved from her pocket money.

The bus swerved into her street and Shivani got in, her eyes searching for him.

Nivin Kochunni, Class 12 B.

It was not that Nivin Kochunni did not know that Shivani Ramachandran of Class 9 B existed. Both of them were Malayalees outside of Kerala and it was only natural that they should know each other. In Saraswati Valley School, Chennai, Shivani and Nivin bumped into each other unfailingly every year when it was time for Onam celebrations and some girls were required to dance around flower patterns in off-white sarees and some boys were required to beat drums in shirt-*mundu*.

Unlike Bella Swan, Shivani belonged to the I-totally-deserve-the-hottest-boy-in-school team. She'd taken many constructive steps to make Nivin Kochunni aware of her presence too.

For example, she'd asked him for his old textbooks so she could save money studying second-hand books. At that point, Shivani had been sure that convincing Nivin that she was dirt poor would make her shine in his eyes. Pretending to be poor was one of Shivani's favourite childhood games at any rate.

She had fond memories of sitting at the dining table and eating her biryani pretending that it was a bowl of stale gruel, the same one that the unfortunate kids in the comic books she read ate. But Nivin had told her that his textbooks were for his little sister Urmila and sorry-I-cannot-help. He did not seem interested in prolonging the conversation by asking her what her interests were (poetry, Shivani would have said), how she managed to look so hot (genes, Shivani would have said), and if she wanted to grab a cup of coffee with him (yes, Shivani would have said).

Now, as she got into the bus, her eyes scanned the last row where the senior boys usually sat. Ah. There he was. Looking out of the window. His hair mussed by the wind. He hadn't shaved today, Shivani noted, butterflies in her stomach. She really wished AR Rahman had been around to provide the appropriate background score to the emotions jangling in her head. Something throaty and pining. He knew this was her bus stop. Why couldn't he at least look at her? She wasn't that bad looking, was she? Snob.

Or maybe, Shivani reasoned, maybe he was *shy*. Or he was just being a thorough gentleman. British gentleman. Not the type who'd ogle girls, you know? But as she took her seat next to Mandodari (Mandy most times and Mandu when she was being stupid), her best friend, Shivani noticed Nivin's eyes straying towards Vishaka of 11 C, lingering there for a moment and then turning away again. Some gentleman.

Shivani plugged in her earphones and proceeded to listen to Lady Gaga. They were not allowed to carry phones to school but almost everyone did. Most teachers were cool with it as long as your phone was on silent in class and you didn't use it while they were in the middle of imparting wisdom. Shivani was so lost in thought that it took her a while to realise that Mandy was prodding her.

'What?' she asked, stopping the song.

'I got a tattoo,' Mandy whispered.

Shivani raised her left eyebrow in response.

'It's a blue butterfly,' Mandy continued. 'With an 'S' on its belly.'

Shivani wondered for a moment if 'S' stood for 'Shivani'. Eww. But then, she remembered that Mandy's boyfriend was called Stephen.

'Where did you get it?' Shivani asked.

Mandy stuck out her right foot and pulled the sock down to reveal the small butterfly on her ankle.

'Did it hurt?'

'A little,' Mandy smiled. 'Steve loves it.'

Shivani rolled her eyes. Stephen was weird. He was 'into' a number of things that ranged from organic farming to turtle conservation. He was a college student which made him all the more exotic.

Mandy and Stephen had met on Facebook on a group called 'Ppl who luv butterflies' (for real). As far as Shivani knew, Mandy did not especially love butterflies. But Shivani herself was on a group called 'Book Addicts' when she didn't like reading all that much. She'd simply signed up for it so people who saw her profile would think she was an intelligent girl. Not to mention, an attractive one. She was careful not to smile too much in her profile photo – instead, it was a side shot that revealed her now here, now gone dimple. It was a whimsical selfie, Shivani thought. It made her look like an interesting, thoughtful person. Shivani suspected that most people on 'Book Addicts' were on it for reasons similar to hers. While they all shared quotes on reading and how they'd all die if they didn't have a book with them (in a recent poll, all of them voted for 'a lovely book' to the question 'What would you want the most if you were shipwrecked and stranded on an island?'), the discussions on actual books barely took off.

She'd sent Nivin a friend request but he'd royally ignored her. However, extensive Facebook research had told her that Nivin liked girls with short hair. He was in a 'Fans of Lisbeth Salander community' and had gone on about how much he liked the character for not just her behaviour but also her looks. Shivani had not read *The Girl With The Dragon Tattoo* but she'd looked up images online. It had taken her two weeks to decide that she must get a haircut if she were ever to score points with him.

'I got it done in Sammy's. In Adyar,' Mandy said, a tad irritated that Shivani wasn't asking her the questions that she'd hoped she would. Why was she staring at the tattoo like a spaced out cow?

'It's nice, Mands,' Shivani said. 'Real cool.'

'Thanks,' said Mandy, mollified. 'You can get one too. With an 'N'.'

'Shut up,' said Shivani, punching Mandy and laughing along with her. She turned back for a second to see if Nivin was looking at her. Nope. He was staring out of the window, lost in thought. He'd unbuttoned the first two buttons of his shirt, displaying the round-necked white vest that he wore beneath it. It was against the rules to do this, of course. But then, everyone loved Nivin, including the teachers. He'd get away with it.

The bus pulled into the school grounds and the students shuffled out, stuffing their phones into their bags and waving bye to their bus friends. Shivani tried waiting for Nivin to move from the last row so she could stand behind him while getting down from the bus but Mandy's look of exasperation made her get up quickly. Bah.

'Listen,' said Shivani during the interval. 'Will you come with me for a haircut?'

Shivani had been planning to go for it by herself but suddenly, now that the day was here, she didn't feel up to doing it by herself.

'A what?' asked Mandy, looking at her phone.

'A haircut. Will you stop texting for one moment and look at me?' said Shivani in exasperation.

'OK. But what kind of haircut do you want? And won't your folks lose it?'

'A pixie,' said Shivani.

Now she had Mandy's undivided attention.

'Are you crazy?! You want to chop it all off?! Like a boy?'

'Why not? It's my hair,' declared Shivani.

Mandy didn't say much after that. In the evening, the two of them decided to bunk basketball practice.

'Are you sure about this?' Mandy asked, when

they were in an auto rickshaw, on their way to an expensive parlour. Shivani wasn't but she nodded confidently.

'Is this to do with Nivin?' asked Mandy. 'I mean, is this why you're doing this?'

'Stop asking so many questions!' snapped Shivani. She didn't want to imagine what Amma and Ammamma would say when she walked in with her new hair. Appa probably wouldn't notice if she walked in with a new head.

When they reached the parlour, Shivani walked in.

'What would you like?' asked the receptionist, as if this were a restaurant. There was lipstick on her teeth.

'Haircut,' answered Shivani.

'She wants a pixie cut,' said Mandy. She sounded a lot more self-assured than Shivani did.

'OK. Pixie has to be done by one of the seniors. So please wait,' said the receptionist.

Shivani and Mandy sat down in the posh chairs. A woman was getting a face massage while a man was getting his hair coloured.

Shivani caught herself in the mirror. She looked like a frog that was about to die. And oh my god, did she really have that many pimples?

The mirror at home was a lot kinder than this. She tried to imagine herself with really short hair. Why hadn't she thought about this more? What if her hair never grew back after this?

'I think we'd better go,' she whispered to Mandy.

'What?' said Mandy. She was looking at her phone as usual.

'Hello girls. Who's ready?' smiled the receptionist. 'One of our seniors just got done. You can go right in.'

'How ... how much is the haircut?' asked Shivani. 'Do we have to pay now?'

'It's 750 rupees,' said the receptionist. 'And you can pay later.'

Relief washed over Shivani. She could feel the sweat run through her hair in rivulets.

'Oh,' she said. 'Oh. I have only a 500.'

Adithi Rao graduated from Smith College, USA, with a degree in Theatre, and returned to India to work as an assistant director on the Hindi film *Satya*. *Shakuntala & Other Timeless Tales from Ancient India* is her first book for children. *Growing Up in Pandupur* is her second. When the Muse comes knocking, Adithi pens the occasional film script, the rights to one of which have been bought by Aamir Khan Productions Ltd. Over the years, her short stories for children have appeared in anthology collections published by Penguin, Scholastic, Puffin and Zubaan. In her free time, Adithi takes long walks and cooks food that her family politely enjoys.

Chatura Rao is an award-winning journalist and an author. Her books for children and adults have been published by leading publishing houses like Penguin, Bloomsbury, Scholastic, Puffin, Ladybird, Young Zubaan and Tulika. Her most recent books are *A Blueprint for Love*, for adults, and *Gone Grandmother*, a picture book for children.

Chatura teaches creative writing to children at Prithvi Theatre, Mumbai, in summer. Her world, like her city, is always "Under Construction"!

Devika Rangachari is a children's writer with several award-winning books to her credit. Her book, *Queen of Ice* (Duckbill), was on the White Ravens list of the best children's books from around the world in 2015. She is also currently engaged in post-doctoral research in gender history.

Jane De Suza is a leading humour writer; her latest books *Happily Never After* and *SuperZero and the Clone Crisis* have both been ranked among Amazon's most memorable books. Her earlier books include the detective-comedy *The Spy Who Lost her Head* and the best-selling *SuperZero* series for children. Jane is a management grad from XLRI, has been Creative Director at leading advertising agencies across India, and writes for publications across the world.

Nalini Sorensen is a children's author, who loves spending time with children and looking at the world through the wonder of their eyes. Her other books include *The Star That Saved the Day, Dada's Useless Present, Alphabet Dress-up* and *Number March*. She is a co-author of *Gifts of Teaching* and *Memories from the Road,* and has written readers for schools in India, and stories for children's magazines. Nalini grew up in Mumbai, but currently lives in Melbourne with her husband and two sons.

Sampurna Chattarji is a poet, novelist and translator who has written 14 books. These include *Wordygurdyboom!* (Puffin Classics, 2008); *The Fried Frog and other Funny Freaky Foodie Feisty Poems* (Scholastic, 2009); her translation of the *Selected Poems* of Joy Goswami (Harper Perennial, 2014); and her book-length sequence of poems, *Space Gulliver: Chronicles of an Alien* (HarperCollins, 2015). Find out more at https://sampurnachattarji.wordpress.com/

Sowmya Rajendran has written books for children of all age groups, from picture books for the very young to young adult fiction. She was awarded the Sahitya Akademi's Bal Sahitya Puraskar for her novel *Mayil Will Not Be Quiet* in 2015. Sowmya currently works with *The News Minute*, writing on gender, culture, and cinema. She lives in Pune.

FLIPPED

SCARY STORIES

Boo!

HarperCollins*Children's*Books

First published in India in 2017 by HarperCollins Children's Books
An imprint of HarperCollins *Publishers*
A-75, Sector 57, Noida, Uttar Pradesh 201301, India
www.harpercollins.co.in

2 4 6 8 10 9 7 5 3 1

Anthology copyright © HarperCollins *Publishers* India

Copyright for individual pieces vests with the authors.

P-ISBN: 978-93-5277-436-4

The contributors assert the moral right
to be identified as the authors of this work.

All rights reserved. No part of this publication may be reproduced,
stored in a retrieval system, or transmitted, in any form or by any means,
electronic, mechanical, photocopying, recording or otherwise,
without the prior permission of the publishers.

Typeset in Candara 12 pt/15.9 by Ram Das Lal, New Delhi (NCR)

Printed and bound at
Replika Press Pvt. Ltd.

CONTENTS

OF GRAVE IMPORTANCE

Adithi Rao

They followed the ball's trajectory through the sky with dismayed eyes, knowing it was lost even before it sailed over the compound wall of the landfill at the far end of the street. Nobody would approach the landfill. Not to retrieve balls, not for anything.

The stench was too terrible.

The boys looked at each other glumly. Then, by tacit agreement, they shouldered their bats and went home.

Now Ethan remained standing alone in the street in the failing light. The others didn't call to him to catch up. It was as if he wasn't there.

1

They were guilty about losing his ball—again— and didn't want to look him in the eye.

Daddy would be disappointed. He would not scold, he would only look at Ethan quietly and turn away. For, this was the eighteenth ball in two months that had been swallowed up by the landfill. Daddy barely earned enough to keep food on the table for the family. There was Daddy and his parents Eliza and Ebenezer, his widowed sister Agnes and her baby daughter Clarissa, Mama and Ethan. All of them squeezed into the tiny three-room cottage on Carter road, in the little Anglo-Indian town of Oorgaum.

Life was not easy for the Robertsons. But it was peppered with happy moments, because they were a loving family. Ethan was a strange child. He got along better with Grandpa Ebenezer than he did with the children in his street. But Daddy wanted him to go outside and play like the other boys did, and so he bought all those cricket balls for his son with the money he could not afford, just so the others would include Ethan in their games.

That night, Ethan couldn't sleep. He kept thinking about the landfill. If only he could muster up the courage to go in there and retrieve them

... Surely he would be able to find at least five or six!

His heart began to thump with fear and excitement.

'I won't tell Daddy,' he thought. 'Instead, I'll try and get in there somehow. Somehow ...'

The next day was Sunday. Ethan stayed home from Church, pleading a headache. When the others had left, he quickly swapped his pyjamas for a pair of trousers and an old t-shirt. Then he raided Grandpa Ebenezer's cupboard and pulled out a large pocket handkerchief. He tipped some of Aunty Agnes' perfume into it and glanced at the clock.

9:23 a.m.

He only had an hour. He would have to hurry. Slamming the door shut behind him, he ran out into the lane.

There was nobody about. Everybody from the neighbourhood had gone to church. All except ...

'Good morning, Mr Jacob,' mumbled Ethan, keeping his eyes down and quickening his pace. He felt a chill pass over him. Nervously, his eyes strayed to the man in the chair, in the front yard of the crumbling old house. Jacob was looking at Ethan. Just looking. Grey, expressionless eyes—

like the eyes of a dead man—followed Ethan as he hurried past the gate.

Ethan touched the perfumed handkerchief to his nose to block out the smell that emanated from the Jacob residence. It was not the smell of alcohol (which Mr Jacob consumed all day long). Not even the odour of the man's unwashed body. This was the smell of despair.

The smell of ... Death.

How did Ethan know this? How could a boy of eleven, who in his living memory had never even attended a funeral, know what death smelt like? There was no explanation. He just knew, that's all.

At the end of Carter road, he made a right onto Laburnum Avenue. There might have been laburnum trees growing here at one time. There weren't any more. Directly ahead of Ethan was the tall wall of the landfill. His steps faltered. He stared at the stone bricks in the wall, broken and cracked in places, a crevice here, an outhang there. Footholds and handholds, if only he dared to seize them. Suddenly a breeze stirred and drifted his way. It brought with it the stench from the landfill, so powerful that his head spun and he gagged. He staggered away to lean against

the fence of a vacant plot, trying to pull himself together.

'Think of the ball. Just think of the ball. You owe it to Daddy,' Ethan thought over and over like a mantra. Then he raised his head and took a deep breath, filling his lungs with fresh air while it was still available.

Squaring his thin shoulders, Ethan covered his nose with Grandpa Ebenezer's handkerchief and secured the ends behind his head into a firm knot. Now his nose would be protected and his hands free for the climb.

Ethan groped blindly for crevices, painstakingly hauling himself up the wall by degrees. One slip and the fall was fifteen feet.

He had nearly reached the top. Suddenly something grabbed his arm and hauled him over the wall. His blood froze and a scream died in his throat. He went hurtling down the other side, expecting to hit his head on the ground or land in a pile of rotting garbage.

Instead, he found himself standing in the soft grass, face to face with an old man with twinkling eyes.

'At last somebody came to visit! The name's Abercrombie,' he grinned.

Ethan stared at him, speechless. In place of the garbage was a beautiful garden, profuse with dense trees and fragrant flowers.

'What you wearing that for, Ethan?' demanded Abercrombie, and yanked off the handkerchief covering Ethan's nose.

'Hey! That's—'

'Ebenezer's, I know. The old thief!' chuckled Abercrombie, pocketing the handkerchief. 'He owed me one. Borrowed mine to bandage up a bruised knee when we were in school together, and never returned it!'

'Er ... Sir?'

'Abercrombie.'

'Er ... Abercrombie Sir?'

'Abe. Grandpa Abe,' supplied the old man kindly.

Now Ethan smiled. Grandpa Abe. That sounded right. It seemed to lurk at the back of his tongue like a distant memory.

'Grandpa Abe, where *are* we?' he burst out suddenly. 'And where is the landfill?'

'There's no landfill, boy. That stink around it is just to keep the humans out. Do you know what those little urchins would do to my garden if they entered it? All my flowers would be plucked! All

the fruits would get stolen! Nothing would remain for the bees and the hummingbirds. Why, my poor squirrels would starve!'

Indeed, the place was teeming with life. There were wood creatures everywhere, busy, playful, ravenous.

'How lovely it is here! I wish I could stay forever!' sighed Ethan, his eyes shining. But when he looked at the old man, he found Grandpa Abe watching him sadly.

'There is a lot that you will have to give up on the other side of the wall to move in here,' said the old man gruffly.

'What, the ugly street and dirty sidewalks, and spooky Mr Jacob? I'd give those up in a minute!' laughed Ethan. But Abe only stared at him oddly and turned away.

'Come. I have something of yours.'

Disconcerted by the sudden change in the old man's mood, Ethan followed him to a place where the roses grew particularly densely. Abercrombie led Ethan behind a rock.

'There you go,' he said curtly. 'Take that and get lost.'

Ethan's eyes nearly popped out of his head. In a gunny sack were his eighteen lost cricket balls!

'Thank you, Sir! cried Ethan delightedly. He turned around to see Abercrombie stumping away.

'Use the gate,' the old man mumbled, waving in the direction of a cluster of bougainvillea. Ethan turned to look. When he turned back, Abercrombie was gone.

Ethan picked up the gunny bag and moved to the rusted little gate, that had bougainvillea growing all over it. He fought his way through the undergrowth and pushed open the gate. It didn't look like it had been used for years. He frowned. How did Grandpa Abe get in and out of the garden?

Ethan now found himself standing in the street behind the landfill. He would have to hurry. The family would be home from church soon. He raced down Laburnum Avenue and turned the corner onto Carter Road. As he dashed past the Jacob residence, he saw only an empty chair. Mr Jacob was no longer in it.

Ethan threw open his front gate and burst into the house. They hadn't come home! They were still at church! He crouched over, gasping for breath, the gunny sack with its precious cargo pressed to his heaving stomach. Slowly his breathing

returned to normal. He glanced at the clock.

It was 9:24 a.m.

* * *

The next day was Monday. School was dull as usual. There was nothing to do but try to make sense of fractions in Maths class, or jot down History notes that began with the Tudor kings, and somehow ended up in Oorgaum, which Miss Pitts, the History teacher, was inordinately fond of. Ethan did not see any point in learning that in 1897 a cholera epidemic had hit Oorgaum and killed all the townspeople, or that the British government had sanctioned the building of a new post office in 1923. The fact was that the new post office was now an old post office—a very *old* post office—and had little relevance to Ethan's eleven-year-old life. But Miss Pitts *would* talk, and there was no friendly face on the bench beside him to whisper jokes to or exchange notes with, to relieve the boredom. Ethan did not have any friends at school.

When he got home from school that day, Clarissa was crying. She had been crying monotonously since 11 that morning, a harassed Aunty Agnes informed him. Ethan tossed his

school bag aside and went to Grandma Eliza, who was rocking the baby in her arms and crooning a hymn. Ethan reached for his cousin, who immediately leaned towards him. She wrapped her little arms around his neck and pressed her soft, wet face into his shoulder, where she continued to fuss and whine. Ethan ran out of the house with her.

'Where —?' called Grandma, but Ethan was gone before she could finish her sentence.

He headed straight for the landfill—garden— ignoring his friends who were playing cricket in the street with the ball he had left for them on the side of the road. They, of course, had no idea it was from him. And they had wasted no time in wondering either. Instead, they had caught up the ball with whoops of delight and straight away plunged into a game.

Ethan pushed open the rusty gate beneath the bougainvillea and stepped through it. If this place didn't cheer Clarissa up he didn't know what would. She had forgotten to cry and was looking around with wide-eyed interest. Ethan walked her around the garden, showing her the flowers and the squirrels. Suddenly Clarissa grew excited. She pointed towards the rose bushes and blabbered

happily. Ethan turned and saw Grandpa Abe emerge. He had obviously been pruning his roses. His fingers were muddy, and he dusted them off as he approached the children, grinning. He held out his arms, exclaiming, 'Clarissa!' and the baby jumped into them joyfully.

Ethan stared in surprise. Why was ten-month-old Clarissa, who screamed at the sight of strangers, now greeting this man like an old friend?

'Good boy, Ethan! You've brought the first one!'

Ethan frowned. What did the old man mean? But there was no time to ask, because Clarissa was pointing to those bushes again, indicating her wish to be taken there. The old man walked away in the direction she showed.

'Hey!' cried Ethan after them. And at that moment a jet-black raven swooped down, brushing him over the head with its wings in passing. Ethan gave a start and spun around in time to see the bird vanish into a distant silver oak. When he turned back, Abe and Clarissa were gone.

* * *

Ethan looked everywhere for the baby, calling,

screaming himself hoarse. But nobody answered, no one came. He had lost his little cousin. What would Aunty Agnes say? And Daddy, and Ebenezer and Eliza? Mama rarely struck him, but this time she would skin him alive.

'It's okay. Let her beat me with an iron rod if only it will bring back Clarissa,' he had wept to the darkening sky above the trees of the garden. Night seemed to have fallen suddenly. Dense clouds had gathered overhead. As lightning struck, Ethan cringed. He turned and fled, horrified that his own fear was prompting him to abandon a little baby and run away.

Two hours later when Ethan barged into his house, practically collapsing from terror and exhaustion, the whole family was seated in the living room. They rose to their feet as one as he sobbed out his story.

Ebenezer looked at Eliza, and she nodded gravely. Aunty Agnes was pale but strangely calm. Only his mother was crying softly. Ethan stared about him, bewildered by the family's frightening composure in the face of such a catastrophe.

Daddy now spoke up. 'It is time,' he said softly. 'It is time. Come.'

Ebenezer, Eliza, Peter, Jenny and Agnes quietly

walked towards the front door and stepped out into the rain. Jenny threw one backward glance at her son. In her eyes was a world of love, and a soft smile passed over her wan face. A second later, she too was gone.

Ethan crumpled to the floor, his head spinning. He felt faint, and laid his head down, trying to fight the blackness that threatened to overcome him. After a while, the dizziness slowly receded. The rain was still pouring down outside, and he slowly got to his feet and walked out of the door from which his family had left. The street outside was pitch dark. All the houses in the neighbourhood seemed deserted. Ethan looked around frightened, the hair on the back of his neck prickling. No lights burned in any of the houses in this street. It was as if the world was empty and he was the last human in it.

Lightening streaked across the sky, ripping it apart cruelly. And in that one brief moment of illumination, Ethan saw a man standing motionless, just inches away from him. He screamed, as steely fingers closed over his arm and dragged him away. He passed out then, sinking into blessed oblivion ...

* * *

He came around to a pair of cold, grey eyes staring unblinkingly down at him.

Mr Jacob.

Ethan sat bolt upright, scrambling to the corner of the bed to get as far away from Jacob as possible, looking about him frantically. Involuntarily he shivered, and this brought about an unexpected softening in the man's face.

'G ... Grandpa Ebenezer?' whispered Ethan fearfully. 'Mama?'

Jacob stood up and turned away. In the flickering candlelight, the room looked almost ... beautiful. The walls were a rich honey colour, the sofas old and plush, the portraits on the wall lifelike and ornate. Time seemed to have stood still in here. He expected the stink to hit him, but the place smelled like freshly baked vanilla cake.

Ethan's stomach rumbled audibly, and Jacob's lips twitched. The man walked to the kitchen and returned with a large slice of warm cake. With a furtive glance at Jacob, Ethan took the plate in both hands and ate hungrily. After that he felt better. When he looked up from his empty plate, Jacob was sitting in the chair close to the bed, watching him again.

'Finished?'

Ethan nodded.

'Want more?'

Ethan did, but shook his head.

'Your family ...' said Jacob quietly.

The boy raised his head eagerly. Jacob stood up and held out his hand, and Ethan took it. They left the house together, Jacob holding a lantern to light up their way.

Ethan was not surprised to see them heading for the landfill. Something in him had known that this was where his family had gone. This was where he would have to look for them.

They had entered the rusty gate, and were moving towards the rose bushes. Now the dread began to rise, flooding Ethan's heart and clutching at his throat with demented fingers. A thousand questions died on his tongue. In a blind panic, Ethan tried to wrench his hand out of Jacob's and felt the man's fingers clamp around his wrist like a manacle. He half-led, half-dragged the boy to a knot of roses that seemed to be covering something.

'Be still!' Jacob commanded. Almost against his will, Ethan found himself frozen to the spot. Jacob bent down and pushed aside the mound of leaves that had blown down in the rain. A

flat, stone slab slowly revealed itself. A grave. Somebody's grave. Ethan wanted to back away but his feet had turned to lead.

Jacob broke away a rose branch. Behind it was the head stone. Wordlessly, he raised the lantern.

RIP
Eliza Robertson

It read. And below it were the words:

Beloved wife of late Ebenezer Robertson
Mother of Peter & Agnes
Died: 19th February, 1897

Ethan gasped, and Jacob, unrelenting, dragged him to another half-covered grave. This one bore the inscription:

Here lies Jenny
Beloved wife of late Peter Robertson
&
Mother of Ethan
Resting in the arms of our Lord
Died: March 23rd 1897

Ethan was now sobbing as if his heart would break. 'Let ... let me find Clarissa and t ... take h

... her home. Her p ... parents are d ... dead and s ... so are m ... mine. We only have each other now,' he pleaded.

Jacob looked down at Ethan.

'Do you really need to see more graves to know?' His voice was harsh, but a hint of pity had slipped into it.

Ethan stared at him and shook his head silently. His sobs had subsided now.

Jacob put an arm around him.

'Come,' he said softly. 'It's time to go home.'

Ethan started to walk in the direction of the rusty gate, but felt a tug on his shoulder. He looked up questioningly.

'Not there,' said Jacob, and steered Ethan towards a patch of lilies. Ethan followed, his mind too numb to wonder. They stopped beside another grave. It was a small one this time, smaller than Jenny's.

Ethan frowned. Suddenly he heard Miss Pitts' voice, droning on in the History class that morning. (Had it only been that morning?) 1897, she had said. An epidemic of cholera, she had said. Nobody from the village survived, she had said.

Nobody.

He looked at the headstone and read:

Ethan Peter Robertson

The boy's head jerked up in time to see Jacob disappear into a grave beyond ...

DANIEL AND THE LONG SHADOW

Payal Dhar

The trouble was that nobody believed Daniel. Not about the thing under his bed, nor about the whole shadow business. Daddy was of the opinion that all this *Doctor Who* nonsense was putting ideas in his head. Mummy said that his late-night snacks were giving him gas and therefore bad dreams. Not even his best friend Vivek believed him. But in the end it didn't matter.

The first time Daniel heard anything, he didn't think much of it – perhaps a sound from outside. It was almost midnight, everyone was asleep. He was awake, though, reading a book. It was called

Gangsta Granny, about a boy with a grandmother who was an international jewel thief and wanted to steal the historic jewels of the British kings and queens. Daniel was loving the book, because he liked to imagine that it was about his own granny, who lived in London.

A good book always made Daniel hungry, and he remembered that there were some new chocolate biscuits in the kitchen that would be an excellent accompaniment to his midnight reading. He pushed his covers away and jumped out of bed. Something slithered on the floor and he looked down in surprise. But there was nothing, just a corner of his sheet trailing on the ground.

The room was full of shadows, soft shadows resting gently on the edge of the warm, yellow glow cast by the bedside lamp at the head of Daniel's bed. It was the familiar light-and-shadow that made him feel safe and warm. Then he heard a low hum. It was almost musical, like someone singing.

A stirring of unease gripped Daniel momentarily. The back of his neck bristled, making a shiver run down his spine. He had a strong feeling that something was off. No sooner did he become

aware of the musical sound than it was gone again, his room returning to the quiet stillness of the night. Everything was calm and quiet once again, so quiet in fact that he wasn't sure if he'd heard anything in the first place.

Daniel swallowed as he backtracked into the corridor. As soon as he was out of his room, his disquiet lifted. The reassuring white light at the furthest end of the corridor that stayed on all night settled around his shoulders in relief. He noticed that he was clutching his book so tightly that he had bent it and there were sweaty finger marks on the cover. He rubbed it on his T-shirt and padded silently to the kitchen to get himself a chocolate biscuit. He was even feeling a little silly now.

But by the time he returned to his room, his unease was back in full strength. Daniel had never been the type of boy who was afraid of the dark. He had only ever been frightened of one thing connected to the darkness, that too when he had been a silly seven-year-old. And that was the underneath of his bed. The idea of this gaping space, harmless and unoffending in the day, but which turned into a yawning shadow of uncertainty in the dark, had always

been hateful. He used to be terrified of his arm or leg hanging over the side of his bed at night because he imagined a horrible creature living in the gaping chasm under his bed who would rush out and grab it.

But I'm ten years old now, Daniel told himself. *I am not afraid. There are no monsters.*

He swallowed and, despite his hammering heart, forced himself to take a step and then another into his room. Try as he might, though, he couldn't push away the anxiety that nagged him anew. It was too strong, the memory of his younger self, waiting for a lumpy, oozing hand to shoot out from under the bed and ... *grab* him!

Without warning, his nerve failed him. With a low moan, he took a running leap towards his bed. He landed on all fours, the biscuit flying from his hand and the book tumbling out too, landing on the floor. A chocolate biscuit didn't seem appetising any more, and there was no way he was getting off to retrieve the book. He huddled under the covers, trying to still his thumping heart.

As for that chilling touch – had he imagined it? It had been just for a moment as his foot had

dangled over the edge of the bed.

* * *

When Daniel woke the next morning, he had no recollection of when he had fallen asleep, or even how. For a moment, he wondered if his creepy night adventure had been real or only a dream. He was just about to conclude that it had been a dream when he felt something hard and sticky by his leg. He reached down to find a chocolate biscuit stuck to his ankle.

So definitely not a dream, he mused. He prised off the biscuit and bit into it – it would be a shame to waste it.

Sunlight was pouring in through the white and yellow curtains, and nothing in his room seemed scary any more. Daniel leaned over and peered underneath his bed. It was empty except for a cardboard box full of old toys and a smattering of dust bunnies.

When the night has come
And the land is dark.

Daniel jerked back up so quickly that his head spun for a moment.

What was that? Where did that come from?

Was it a song? It had been a quiet, low hum, just like last night. But this time he heard it clear and crisp, as though someone was singing it inside his head. If it was a song, he had never heard it before.

And there was something else. Slowly, Daniel bent down, gripped the edge of his bed and peered under it again. The floor underneath was dusty, except for a curving, slender path, as if something had been dragged along it. Or had something slithered through ...

'Daniel, bath!' His mother's voice brought him back to reality with a bump. 'You're late.'

He quickly rammed the rest of the biscuit into his mouth and ran for the bathroom. *Nah, probably made by a broom or something,* he said to himself.

It was almost a relief to pour a mug of warm water over his head. He scrubbed himself well, especially his foot, where the memory of that ice-cold touch still lingered. But however hard he scrubbed and however much water he poured on himself, a vague sense of malaise lingered deep inside. That and the song that refused to leave his head.

* * *

24

Daniel and Vivek stood outside the staff room waiting for their teacher.

> *When the night has come*
> *And the land is dark*
> *And the moon is the only light we'll see*
> *No I won't be afraid, no I won't be afraid.*

The song continued to nag him, now a couple of lines longer. Daniel's head ached and the top of his right foot itched inside his shoes. He wished their teacher would hurry up. It wasn't pleasant standing out in the corridor, with the sun beating down on them from between the wide balcony pillars.

He glanced at Vivek, who was busy worrying a scratch on the pillar. He didn't seem to be bothered by the sun, squinting against it. Daniel turned away from him, facing the staff room door. That was when he noticed something else. He and Vivek were exactly the same height. Yet the L-shaped shadows that ran from their feet along the floor and rose up against the door were not. Vivek's shadow bobbed erratically as he scratched at the pillar. But Daniel's – that was another story.

It pulsed and bubbled, like it was trying to break out of its confines, and it was growing taller and taller and taller. Vivek's shadow was at the level of the door handle, but Daniel's was inching upwards very slowly.

For the first time, Daniel felt afraid.

'Vivek.' He pushed at his friend's shoulder.

'Huh?'

'Look at my shadow?'

Daniel had looked away only for an instant, to get Vivek's attention. But when he turned back to the door, both shadows were normal.

'What about your shadow?' Vivek asked, sounding bored.

'I ... it ... it was there. I saw it! It was long, longer than yours ... and growing ...'

Vivek looked at him like he was insane. For a moment Daniel wondered if he *was* going mad.

Then the door opened and their teacher came out with two piles of exercise books for the boys to carry back to their classroom.

* * *

When dusk fell, Daniel was overcome with a sort of listlessness. At the same time, he was jumpy

and irritable and afraid. He recoiled nervously when his father touched him on the shoulder to ask if he was feeling all right, and he snapped at his little sister Cecelia when she asked if he would play Uno with her.

He had spent the entire day watching his shadow, waiting for it to misbehave again. From the corners of his vision he could sense that whenever he wasn't looking at it directly, his shadow fought and pulsed and grew. It grew longer and longer, like a naughty child trying to venture free from its mother and going off where it wasn't supposed to. And whenever Daniel turned his head to catch it misbehaving, it snapped back into place.

The song hummed continuously in his head, as mental background music to all his thoughts. He had no control over it. He tried to sing other songs, but it was all in vain. It had now progressed to a chorus:

So darlin', darlin', stand by me, oh stand by me
Oh stand by me, stand by me.

'You've been very quiet tonight,' his father observed. 'And you haven't touched your food.'

Daniel looked down at the chapatti on his plate. He had torn out a piece, but it was floating on the bowl of dal aimlessly. The thought of putting it in his mouth made him sick. The thought of having to go to his room and stay there alone ...

But what could he say? 'There's something under my bed' seemed like something Cecelia, who was six, would have a problem about.

'There's something wrong with my shadow,' he burst out.

His parents stopped eating and turned to him. Even Cecelia stared at him.

'Your what?' his mother asked.

'It's ...' This time, as he watched it, his shadow grew a long extension like an arm. From its end, smaller extensions shot out till it took the shape of a hand, which waggled a finger at Daniel in reprimand.

'Look!' he cried, pointing.

By the time everyone looked at the floor, the shadow was back to normal. But inside his head the chorus rose to a thundering crescendo:

... oh stand by me
Stand by me, stand by me, stand by me, STAND

BY ME ...

'Stop!' cried Daniel, putting his hands over his ears.

It was clear that except for Daniel, nobody could hear anything else. His mother looked slightly worried, but his father tch-ed irritably.

'No more late-night TV shows for you,' he said.

'Leave your food. Go to bed. I'll get you some carbo veg to settle your stomach,' his mother said.

'No,' whispered Daniel. Bed was the last place he wanted to go. But he didn't have a choice.

This time the song in his head was soft, like it was trying to be reassuring.

Stand by me, oh stand by me.

Who are you? Daniel asked loudly in his head. And it answered:

Stand by me ...

Fear gripped Daniel. His right foot felt so cold, like it was frozen. The coldness started to spread, till it flowed through his torso, bled into his shoulders and arms, and filled his head. Even the tips of his ears were cold.

'I don't want to sleep in my room,' said Daniel softly. His eyes were hurting, he knew he was going to cry. He looked down at his lap as a big fat tear dropped down on to his leg.

He heard a chair being scraped back, then his mother's voice. 'Bed. I'll come with you.'

Daniel had no choice but to let himself be led to his room. He was shivering.

'Do you have a fever?' his mum asked, a hand resting on his forehead momentarily. She hissed in surprise, 'You're so cold. You get into bed right now.'

So darlin', darlin', stand by me, oh stand by me
Oh stand by me, stand by me.

Daniel clapped his hands over his ears again. *All right, all right! Anything!* he yelled, inside his head.

'What's the matter? Does it hurt?' his mother sounded worried.

A funny thing happened just then – odd-funny, not ha-ha funny. The dread that had seeped into the middle of his bones lifted without warning and he felt a whole lot better. Just like that, as if a switch had been flipped from the 'Feeling

Horrible' position to 'All Better Now'. The song was gone too.

'No. Nothing hurts,' said Daniel.

He sat down on his bed with a bump. The silence in his head was resounding.

* * *

Daniel hated games period. It wasn't that he was bad at sports, it was more to do with Ms Moses. She had a mean streak about her and she took all the fun out of games, whether it was kho-kho, mass PT, basketball or just exercises.

'What are you? Boy or stick insect?' she goaded, watching Daniel trying to do push-ups. 'Don't you get to eat at home?'

Ordinarily, that should have been a cue for his classmates to start sniggering. But each and every one of them in class 5B had been stung too many times by Ms Moses' poisonous tongue, which had resulted in an unlikely bond of solidarity. So nobody moved, nobody said anything.

'Answer my question – do you get to eat at home?' Ms Moses demanded.

'Yes, ma'am,' Daniel muttered.

'Then prove it!' she thundered.

Daniel glared at Ms Moses through hooded eyelids and got on to his hands and feet. Even before he flicked his eyes to see, he knew that Ms Moses was standing on his shadow – he could sense it. Her shins were placed squarely within the black silhouette that was the shadow of his head.

It didn't take more than a second, but to Daniel it played out like a satisfying scene from a well-directed movie. Inside the shadow of his head, two rows of something long and sharp blossomed, blacker than the dark outline that was ordinarily visible. They positioned themselves on two sides of Ms Moses' shin, paused for a moment, almost theatrically, and then closed with the silent snarl of an invisible phantom and the military precision of heavy-duty steel jaws.

Ms Moses screamed, making the children scatter in alarm. She fell to the ground, clutching her leg, howling with pain. The children watched with horrified fascination as she bellowed curses that turned the air blue around her.

'Go and get some help, you moronic brats!' she screeched, tears running down her face.

But the children stood, rooted to wherever

they were, unsure of what to do. Only Daniel smiled.

Stand by me? he said to himself.

The long shadow nodded. Daniel even suspected it winked.

WHEN I WAS A LITTLE GIRL

Shabnam Minwalla

When I was a little girl—and then a not-so-little girl—we had fixed plans for the summer holidays. Every year, we spent ten days at a friend's bungalow in Mahabaleshwar.

We ate enormous breakfasts and ran around the garden, plucking flowers and getting scratched by the dry grass and poky bushes. Sometimes we visited strawberry farms where we stuffed our baskets and ourselves till we were pink and sticky. Sometimes we went on horse rides through the misty forests, imagining snakes and leopards behind every tree.

Sometimes we piled into cars and drove to one of the famous 'points' – especially those known for their echoes. Many of these peaks and points were associated with people who had plunged down the hillside and met tragic deaths.

We shuddered over those long-ago tragedies. But as we were five of us, we felt safe. Neither ghosts nor wild animals would take on such a rowdy, cocky bunch of children. Our loud quarrels and sunny laughter held even the thick fogs at bay.

Then one year, our friends decided to spend the summer in Singapore. For a few days my family considered holidaying in Ooty and Goa, but finally decided to return to the misty familiarity of 'Mahabs'.

Only, this time we would have to stay in a hotel. And, it would be just my parents, my brother and me. My brother was younger than me – and a ten-year-old Spiderman fan is of little use to a dreamy twelve-year-old girl.

'We can hire bicycles from the bazaar ... and we can buy jam,' my mother said, as the bus trundled up the mountains and the air outside got cooler and thinner. 'And there are bound to

be other children at the hotel, with whom you can play.'

My mother had found the hotel by asking around. Somebody had mentioned an old Parsi bungalow that had recently been converted into a small, secluded hotel. It seemed perfect. We didn't have money for a fancy hotel with room service and mini bars and big signboards. 'It's supposed to be very atmospheric and away from the crowds,' my mother said.

This was one of the reasons why we found ourselves on a narrow, uphill path, well after the sun had set. The hotel was supposed to be twenty minutes away from the bus stop; but an hour later, we were still dragging our suitcases, squabbling and trying to locate Hotel Hillside.

We had found the final landmark of Vijay Cold Drinks, but nobody had mentioned that the road forked after that. First we took the right fork, which seemed wider and more welcoming. But the only gates we could see were locked, and all the bungalows were dark.

So we backtracked and took the left fork, while my mother tried to cheer us up by reciting, 'The Road Not Taken'.

The poem didn't help.

Mahabaleshwar's version of the road not taken was narrow and uneven. Unfriendly branches reached out and clawed at our arms and bags. The darkness was thick and impenetrable – the kind you only experience on mountain roads.

The silence was complete – broken only by our shrill voices. We hadn't met a soul in the last fifteen minutes. Suddenly, the wild animals and menacing ghosts of holidays past seemed to be closing in on us.

I burst into tears. Then I shrieked.

Standing right in front of us was a girl my age. She was bundled up in a shawl or blanket and was looking at us from behind a low wall.

'Oh, we are so relieved to see someone,' my mother gasped. 'Are your parents here?'

The girl stared with blank eyes in a chalky white face.

'Maybe you can help us,' my mother said, desperate. 'Do you know where Hotel Hillside is?'

The girl stared again.

'Hotel Hillside, Frainy Villa,' my mother repeated, very slowly.

The girl looked up with sudden surprise. Slowly, she pulled out her hand from under her shawl and pointed at a little clearing ahead.

My mother thanked her, smiled and asked, 'Are you staying here? It will be nice if you and Mansi can play together, won't it Mansi?'

I did a mental eye-roll and tried to smile. But it was a wasted effort. The girl was looking at the clearing. In the faint moonlight, we could make out a garden and a squat bungalow.

'It doesn't look like a hotel,' my father protested. 'It's completely dark.'

'So?' my mother snapped, 'Do you have any better ideas?'

'I'm going to check,' my brother said, running in the direction of the clearing. 'I'm hungry.'

My parents rushed behind him and the crunch of dry leaves almost drowned out the whisper.

'... play with the dolls.'

Puzzled, I turned to look at the girl. But she had turned away and was melting into the black night.

'Please play with the dolls? Don't play with the dolls? What did she say?' I wondered. 'What dolls? And which twelve-year-old plays with dolls anyway?'

By the time I reached the door of the bungalow, everybody was looking happier. We'd

38

actually managed to find the hotel in the midst of a power cut. Our dinner was ready and Rakesh, the young man who ran the place, handed us a torch and welcomed us to Hotel Hillside.

My mother switched on the torch as we entered, and we saw an old-fashioned living room with glass-fronted cabinets, plump sofas and a vast dining table ringed by heavy, wooden chairs. Our dinner was sitting on the table in a steel tiffin box.

'My mother is the cook,' Rakesh explained in Marathi. 'She cooks at home and I bring the food for you.'

'She doesn't cook here?' my father asked. He had been planning to order hot pakodas and tea through the day. That was his idea of the perfect holiday.

'She doesn't like … she doesn't like this kitchen,' Rakesh mumbled, and pointed to two doors leading away from the old-fashioned living room. 'These are your rooms.'

'And where are the other rooms?' my father asked.

Rakesh indicated a staircase. 'There are three rooms upstairs, but nobody else is staying here

now. I come early every morning and stay till you finish your dinner.'

'Shouldn't somebody be here at night?' my father demanded.

'My mother ... old ... alone,' Rakesh muttered, sounding evasive. 'If you need anything at night, you can phone and I will come.'

My father looked displeased, and my mother jumped in. 'That means we have the place to ourselves,' she laughed, moving her torch around. 'What an adventure. So much character.'

The beam of the torch danced over porcelain cups and some hideous glass vases in the glass cabinet before it shone on the round, rosy face of a doll. It was a baby doll with a white, frilly bonnet, plump cheeks and a beckoning hand. But in the flat light of the torch, its eyes appeared like dark holes – as though pressed in by angry thumbs.

I felt a stab of fear and again I heard those strange words, '... play with the dolls.'

Just then the lights came on in Frainy Villa. We hurried to get settled and eat dinner, and I forgot all about the baby doll and my moment of terror.

Over the next few days we did all the usual

hill station things. We cycled, ate Swiss Rolls from the cake shop and explored the area around Hotel Hillside. Or rather Frainy Villa, as everybody insisted on calling it.

Frainy, we soon found out, had been the only daughter of a rich Parsi family. She was a frail child, so her parents bought a bungalow in Mahabaleshwar and brought her here every year. Then one night—when she was about twelve— she left her bed and went outside. They found her in the morning, lying lifeless beneath a cliff.

'Nobody understood why she had left her bed in the middle of the night or climbed those rocks,' the grey-haired woman at Gladys Cake Shop said with disapproval. 'It was very disturbing. We had heard things, but no one expected this.'

My mother glanced at me, worried about my 'overactive imagination'. She tried to change the topic, but the grey-haired woman nodded at me. 'You should be careful,' she said, as though wandering about at night was an infectious ailment that twelve-year-old girls caught. 'So many strange stories one hears.'

The story of Frainy disturbed me. I wondered if I was sleeping in her bed. If I was climbing her favourite tree. But badminton, cakes and

strawberries helped me push away the faded events of forty years ago.

My brother and I enjoyed the pretty, overgrown garden. But the bungalow itself was a bit gloomy and eerie, especially after dusk. One of those places with huge four-poster beds, yellowing mirrors and dim light bulbs. Our bedroom, especially, seemed designed to block the sun and sky. A dark green creeper snaked and coiled across much of the window.

About a week into our holiday, I got a bad cold. I spent some time reading my Nancy Drew mystery. Then I wandered into the living room and peered into the glass-fronted cupboards with their strange knick-knacks. Pewter jugs, crystal animals, carved wooden boxes. And the dolls.

There was the baby doll that I'd noticed on the first day. Then another doll with black hair and a yellow checked dress. And a third doll with golden hair and a flouncy pink dress. All three had pale, watchful eyes.

I don't like dolls. I didn't play with them when I was three, and I certainly wouldn't play with them when I was twelve. Still, something made me tug at the cabinet door. It was tightly jammed, so I

yanked again. And again. And, suddenly, with a loud grunt, the door opened and I found myself face to face with the dolls.

Up close, they looked battered and tired. The baby doll actually had mud on its chubby hand. I wondered why anybody would display them in a glass cabinet in a living room.

My brother sauntered into the room just then. 'Creeeeeepy,' he exclaimed, staring at the baby doll. 'If I met a baby who looked like that I would move to the moon.'

'Shhh,' I said, though I agreed with him. There was something about the baby doll, with its pale grey eyes, that was really unpleasant.

My brother looked at me with disgust. 'It's a doll,' he said. 'It can't hear you.'

'I know that,' I snapped. But actually, I wasn't so sure.

Though the baby beckoned with its upraised hand, I picked up the golden-haired doll instead. She had a sweet, sad expression and I wondered if she had belonged to Frainy. The thought spooked me, and I quickly replaced her on the shelf. I closed the cabinet door but it refused to shut snugly.

'Oh, forget it,' I thought. The dust released by that long-neglected cabinet had made me feel

sicker than ever. I returned to the four-poster bed in the dim bedroom and fell asleep.

By evening I was feverish and uneasy. 'You go and buy Chocobars,' I told my parents with a martyrish air. 'I'll just rest.'

'Okay,' my mother agreed. 'We'll be back in an hour. We'll get you some Lemon Roll to cheer you up.'

I slumped on the living room sofa, drifting in and out of a grey, cotton-woolly sleep, when I heard the sound.

A giggle. Loud enough to jerk me awake.

Blinking, I looked around.

Inside, the room was almost dark. Outside, a fog was rolling in. I jumped to my feet just as something fell behind me with a loud crash. This was followed by another giggle.

Screaming frantically, I tried to find the light switch. Rakesh got there before me and the room was bathed in a golden glow.

'What happened? Why were you screaming?' Rakesh asked.

'Somebody laughed ...' I mumbled in my broken Marathi. 'Something fell.'

'Laughed?' Rakesh repeated blankly. 'Who laughed? Maybe somebody on the road?'

We looked around the room. Everything was exactly as it should be. Except that the glass door of the cabinet had swung open. Instead of three dolls, there were only two on the shelf. The black-haired doll in the checked dress lay smashed on the floor.

Rakesh kept shooting me peculiar looks. He swept up the shards of porcelain and the corpse of the doll and threw it all away.

'Who did the dolls belong to?' I asked, rather worried.

Rakesh just shrugged.

'Had they once belonged to Frainy?'

Rakesh pursed his lips and left the room. He seemed upset.

My parents came in a few minutes later. I told them about the broken doll, and my mother, playing detective, decided that the accident must have been caused by a mouse.

Except that mice don't giggle.

I was feverish at night and kept hearing babyish gurgles and chuckles in my sleep. The next morning, when nobody was watching, I picked up the baby doll and stuffed it into a large wooden cupboard with a stout lock. I felt a bit foolish but much happier.

45

Overnight, Mahabaleshwar had turned foggy and damp. 'We came at the right time,' my father remarked. 'I think the rains will begin soon. Good we are leaving in two days.'

Before going to bed that night, I checked that the wooden cupboard was firmly locked. Then I fell into the deep, dreamless sleep of recovery. So I was groggy and disoriented when an urgent voice whispered, 'Mansi, Mansi. Hurry.'

'What, what?' I asked, sitting up, confused and dizzy.

'Hurry,' my brother said, already outside the bedroom door. 'I just saw mummy walking across the garden. Where is she going? Hurry. I'm afraid. I'm waiting for you in the garden.'

I grabbed a woolen shawl, wore my flipflops and ran outside – quaking with cold and fear. 'Shouldn't we call papa? Take a torch?' I wailed.

'Hurry, hurry,' my brother called. 'No time. Follow me. I think I saw her walking uphill.'

'Why?' I asked. However hard I tried to stop myself, I imagined Frainy walking up the same path forty years ago. 'Wait for me Ayaan.'

I couldn't see my brother through the fog, but could hear the crunch of dried leaves. I had lost all sense of direction and kept stumbling into

trees and rocks. Then after about ten minutes, the trees seemed to fall away and the path became steep. The terrors of the last few days clogged my head, so that I could barely breathe. 'Mummy,' I screamed as I scrambled uphill. 'Ayaan. Please. Where are you?'

Ayaan's footsteps stopped. 'You've gone off the road,' he said softly. 'Just walk about five or six steps ahead. That's all.'

I started walking ahead, one slow step after another. The ground seemed flatter now, and suddenly free of thorns and bushes. 'Where is mummy?' I sobbed.

There was silence for a second. And then on that cold, rocky hillside blanketed in impenetrable fog, I heard the most chilling sound in the world.

A soft, stifled giggle.

'Only two more steps,' my brother urged. 'Only two more steps and you'll be safe.'

I tried to force my legs to obey. I lifted one leg and halted midstep. There was a frantic crunch of leaves, the sound of a scuffle and a sharp, short scream.

'Ayaan? Mummy?' I shrieked, and in that silence an echo replied, 'aaaaan, maaaameee, eeeeeeee.'

'Ayaaaaaan,' I screamed again, and again heard the telltale 'aaaaaaan.'

I knew then—without the faintest doubt—that I was at the brink of a valley. A single step might send me hurtling to my death.

I sank down sobbing, and for the rest of the night remained as still as the mountain.

'Ayaan,' I screamed every half hour. But the only answer I received was from the waiting valley.

They found me soon after dawn, huddled in a brown shawl, unable to speak or walk. I was perched at the very edge of a precipice. One step more and I would have tumbled down to my death.

Like the golden-haired doll who lay in fragments at the bottom of the cliff face. A scatter of pink and gold.

Ayaan was fine. In fact, he was the first one to reach me when the search party arrived.

'Why shouldn't I be fine?' he asked, when I started hugging him and crying. 'You were the one who climbed hills in the middle of the night.'

Ayaan had woken up for water at about 5 a.m. and realised that I was not in my bed. He remembered the story of Frainy, got alarmed

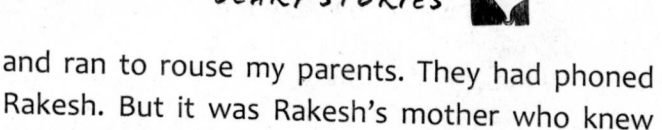

and ran to rouse my parents. They had phoned Rakesh. But it was Rakesh's mother who knew where to go.

Without a moment's hesitation, she had led them up the hill to the cliff from where Frainy had fallen to her death. And there they found me. Mute with cold and terror. But alive.

'Frainy saved me,' I told my parents again and again after we reached the hotel. 'She must have pushed the doll off the cliff.'

'Maybe,' my mother said. She looked bewildered. She was wondering if this was another case of an over-active imagination.

Rakesh's mother had just entered the room with mugs of steaming tea and plates of toast. She heard my words and put the tray down with an angry bang.

'Maybe you saved yourself,' she said.

'But ... but ...' I stammered. 'It must have been Frainy. I think the dolls must have led her to her death so she wanted to save me ...'

'I know that it's not right to speak ill of the dead,' Rakesh's mother spoke in rapid-fire Marathi. 'But for this once, I'm going to speak my mind. I knew Frainy Shroff. My mother was her maid. My father was the gardener here for

many years. So I know that ... that Frainy was not a nice girl.'

'That poor child,' my mother protested, looking around nervously.

'Why do you think they hid her away in Mahabaleshwar?' Rakesh's mother continued, ignoring the interruption. 'We may be uneducated villagers but we know a few things. Her parents adored her. But even they realised that Frainy wasn't sick in her body, she was sick in her mind. She lied. She knew things that small girls don't usually know. I once saw her set a kitten's tail on fire.'

'She could imitate everybody, and used that to get everyone in trouble. Those dolls were always with her. She played terrible games with them. Games about death and destruction. She liked to hurt people. She killed small animals. She hurt her playmates. She carried with her a sense of evil.'

'But she's been dead for years,' my father said.

'Yes. But the evil she created remained. I could feel it every time I stepped into this bungalow. A darkness. A badness. Ever since they opened the hotel I've been fearing something like this.

What I didn't know was that the evil had entered the dolls.'

'Maybe she regrets what she did. Maybe, by saving Mansi she's trying to correct things,' my mother said. Like me, she had been imagining Frainy as a Poor Little Rich Girl Who Died Young.

Rakesh's mother just shrugged. 'Believe what you want. But remember that I knew Frainy, you didn't.'

There was nothing left to say. We finished breakfast, packed our bags and loaded up the taxi. We were desperate to get home.

Before we left, though, there was one thing I needed to do. Trembling, I went to the wooden cupboard. It was firmly locked, but when I turned the key I knew exactly what I would find. Nothing.

The baby doll was gone.

I felt sick. Somewhere the evil still lurked.

Minutes later, our taxi drove out of the garden of Frainy Villa towards the crowds and normalcy of Bombay. As we passed the wall where we had met the girl with the dark shawl, I thought I saw a figure in the fog.

And that is where my story ends.

All that remains are the questions that

have haunted me ever since. And a couple of postscripts.

Hotel Hillside shut down just a few months after we visited. Frainy Villa was locked up and left to the mercy of creepers and termites.

Finally, there is the unsettling observation that my brother made a couple of weeks ago. He was visiting from Detroit, and we were chatting after dinner when he said suddenly, 'There's one thing I never told you about that morning in Mahabaleshwar. When we found you at the edge of the cliff that morning, I didn't recognise you for a moment. You looked exactly like that girl in the shawl that we met on out first night in Mahabaleshwar. The same shawl. The same white face. The same blank expression. But I don't know if it means anything.'

I didn't know either. And I really don't want to.

WINNER TAKES IT ALL

Lubaina Bandukwala

'Aryan, your nose is looking really long today.'

'Yeah, Pinocchio's nose grew longer because he told lies; Aryan's grows longer because he boasts so much!'

'Shut up! Guys, there is nothing wrong with my nose. Leave me alone,' said Aryan shoving off the hands that tried to turn his face towards them.

'We are the champions!' 'No, I am the champion!' the strains of the boys' mocking chant followed Aryan as he walked away from class.

'Losers!' He said to himself. 'Yes of course, I, Aryan Ahuja, am a champion – ace at studies, champ at sports, unbeatable debate king. They are just a bunch of losers!'

And yet he was worried. 'My nose? I wonder, could it have ...' With a growing sense of dread he went to the washroom and looked cautiously into the mirror. Yes. It was not just longer. It was a different shape. As he touched a finger to his nose, fear rose like a physical thing in his throat.

Slinging his backpack over his shoulder he walked out of the school and almost ran to his house that was just ten minutes away. Ignoring his mom's 'Hi Aryan, is that you?' he ran up the stairs two at a time and burst into his room. On his desk lay a pencil sketch of his face – with his nose longer than usual, just like it was now on his face. He grabbed the sketch-pad and tore off the sheet. Ripping it into bits he threw it out of the window. As the bits of paper fluttered down to the ground, Aryan saw him again, standing under the tree looking up at his window. With that smug infuriating malicious half smile playing on his lips.

Taking a deep breath, he turned back to his desk. In the quiet room, there was suddenly an even quieter menace. Even as he looked at his desk, Aryan knew what he would see. Before his eyes, the sketch re-appeared on the blank sheet of paper, feature by feature, altered nose and all.

'You promised ...'

'You are mine ...'

The words sounding raspy and amused swirled around in his head.

Aryan covered his face and let out a soundless scream. What had he done? He was good at everything, why had he not accepted that Meher was better than him in art? But no, he had to ace everything. At any cost.

So he'd added a few brush strokes to her magnificent oil painting. Rubbed an oil stain on her pencil sketch. Yes, made her lose points. But she was still a better artist than him. And since they were neck to neck with all other things, it seemed that she would win the all-rounder prize.

No, he had to win. At any cost. That was the thought uppermost on his mind as he walked into a tiny art store that weekend in search of charcoal pencils. He had never seen the store before. His feet seemed to have led him automatically to it. And before he knew it he was standing before a tall thin man with a long thin face. He had a mole on his chin and an odd scar on his eyebrow. His eyes were deep black and sunken, but oddly knowing. On his lips played a small malicious smile.

'Ah what have we got here? A winner.'

Aryan started, 'Sorry?'

'You like to win, it's a good thing. I also like to be a winner.' He gestured to a large photo of himself with a medal, sitting in a frame on the counter.

'Oh! What did you win?'

'Anything. Everything. Against anyone – even yamraj!' the man laughed.

Feeling oddly uneasy, Anand said, 'OK uncle, maybe you don't have what I need. I'll come another time.'

The man put out a seemingly frail hand and held Aryan's arm in a tight grip. Aryan couldn't move his eyes from the man's face.

'How badly do you want to win?' he asked. His voice sharp.

'Badly,' whispered Aryan.

'What are you willing to give up for it?'

'Anything. Everything,' Aryan unconsciously parroted the man's words.

The man smiled wider, 'So you're willing to pay the price.' It was a statement, not a question.

'Oh yes! I want to win at any cost,' said Aryan, as the horrifying picture of Meher getting the Best All Rounder Medal rose in his mind.

'So you need charcoal pencils?' said the man, suddenly letting go.

Aryan blinked at his sudden change of topic. And wondered how the man knew. He hadn't asked him for the pencils as yet.

'Yes. Yes, please.'

Pulling out a box from the drawer under his counter, he said, 'Many a gold medallist has used these pencils of mine. Go ahead, try your luck with them. But if you do win, you will have to pay a price! Remember.'

'Err yes,' said Aryan. This man was weird, he thought, as he took his pencils, paid for them and literally ran out of the shop. And as he left, the man said, 'Remember, you have to pay the price.'

The pencils did in fact bring him luck. They flew across the paper and made him perfect pictures. Faces, places, objects, it was as if the pencils had given him a kind of magic.

And finally, the day of reckoning. Aryan scored the highest in art and that made him the new winner of the all-round medal!

On that day, he decided to go to the small shop and tell the owner that his pencils had indeed helped him win. But when he got to the street on which the shop was, he found it boarded up! He walked up to the paan shop next door and asked, 'Has this store shut down?'

'Almost ten years ago,' replied the paanwala.

'What? But I bought my pencils here two weeks ago!'

'You must be mistaken beta, this store was closed a week after the owner died ten years ago!'

'He died?'

'Yes. Anand was a brilliant artist. He was not only good at art. He was also very good at sports. But he was also very competitive. He had to win. He simply couldn't stand it if anyone won anything. One time he participated in several sports events one after the other, ending with a cross country event and collapsed during the swimming lap. In the end, he lost the biggest match – against death.'

A shiver ran down Aryan's spine. 'Anything. Everything. Against anyone. Even Yamraj!' Who was that man he met, and what did he mean by his words?

'Are you sure the store has been closed for that long?' he asked urgently.

'Arre baba,' replied the paanwala. 'My paan store has been here since the last fifteen years. I know everything that goes on in this area.'

Aryan mumbled his thanks and walked home. He had bought the pencils from the store. But the

paanwala said the store was closed. How come he had found the store open? Had he spoken to a dead man?

'Ready to pay the price?'

There he was. Right in front of him. Smiling his horrible smile.

'Who are you? What do you want from me?' Aryan backed away.

The man reached out and held the boy's chin with long cold fingers and looked into his eyes. His dark strangely empty, yet evil, eyes pierced him. Terrified, Aryan tried to free himself, but his grip was strong. It was as if the air around him had become still, malice and evil seemed to flow out of the man and Aryan felt paralysed by fear.

'I want to win against Yamraj. You agreed to pay the price. The price is you. Just a little mole on your chin, a scar on the eyebrow, the nose just a little longer ... and I will live through you.'

Aryan wrenched himself from the man's grip and ran home.

'You are mine.' The man's words galloped furiously towards Aryan like a predator closing in on its prey.

That night the first of the sketches appeared on his sketch pad. At first it was just with a mole

on the chin. Two days later he saw the scar on the paper. And in the mirror. And everywhere he went, he saw Anand. No one else seemed to see him. He waved to him from beyond the basketball court. He smiled his evil smile across the gates of his home. Turned around to catch his eye as he sat behind in a crowded bus. 'You will pay the price.' The words became louder, stronger and more confident as every little change took place on Aryan's face.

Aryan began to take different routes to school, to tuition and to his friends' house. He managed to trick Anand and almost lost him. When Anand did manage to catch him, his face was distorted with rage. 'You think you can beat me? Remember, I win everything, at any cost!'

On Sunday morning, Aryan felt much better. He hadn't seen Anand in a week. There had been no more sketches or changes to his face. Yes, maybe he, Aryan, had won after all. He put on his running shoes and set off for a long run. His run led him past the main town along smaller roads. He kept looking over his shoulder but there was no one following him.

He finally stopped at the banks of the river that ran into the town. He stood feeling exhilarated. He

had won. He took deep breaths of fresh air. And moved towards the river to splash water on his face. He walked into the water feeling its coolness lapping around his ankles. He wanted to immerse his whole body into its coolness and waded into deeper waters. How he loved the water around his neck. His eyes felt cool as his face disappeared into the water. 'You are mine!' the water seemed to whisper as it closed in over his head.

A few minutes later, a few people by the river saw a man emerge from the water. He was tall, and had a thin face with a mole on the chin and a long nose. There was an odd scar on his eyebrow. And passersby remember noticing that his face seemed to glow triumphantly.

Later that day, it was discovered that Aryan Ahuja was missing. An extensive search was carried out for weeks. But he was never found again.

THE AIRHOSTESS

Sowmya Rajendran

Aman was sleeping when it happened. The plane started shaking and Ammamma clutched his hand in fear. Aman whispered to her that it was okay. Nothing would happen. Planes shook all the time. They were just flying through some bad weather. Nothing would happen. Nothing would happen. Right?

Then the airhostess came towards them. 'Is everything all right?' she asked. The badge on her chest said her name was Nikita. Ni-ki-ta. She had grey eyes and very dark hair. Aman wondered if she was fully Indian. He had a crush on her already and didn't want the journey to end. What was he going to do about his crush? Nothing. Aman was

only fourteen. When you are fourteen, nothing could happen. Nothing could happen. Right?

'She's a little afraid,' Aman said, trying to look like an adult. A proper grown-up. NOT a fourteen-year-old. 'This is her first flight. She's from a village.'

'I am not!' Ammamma shot back, stung. 'I grew up in Hyderabad.'

'See how I distracted you?' Aman asked, grinning.

Ni-ki-ta broke into a smile.

'It will be all right,' she said. 'Just make sure you don't take off your seatbelts.'

She then went to the back of the plane and sat down, following the instructions given by the pilot. Next to Christine, the other airhostess. She was pretty, too, but not like Ni-ki-ta.

By the time the plane landed in Chennai, Ammamma was acting like she'd actually given the pilot flying lessons. 'This plane ... it went so slow,' she said. 'I couldn't feel a thing. No thrills.'

'At your age, thrills might give you a heart attack,' Aman said.

His mother, who'd come to the airport to pick them up, shot him a disapproving look.

'Is this the way to talk to your grandma?' she frowned.

Both Ammamma and Aman ignored her.

On the way back, in the car, Ammamma asked Aman what he thought about Nigitha.

'Ni-ki-ta!' Aman exclaimed, pained.

'Yes, Nigitha. You liked her, no?' said Ammamma. 'I saw you.'

'Saw me do what?' asked Aman, buying time.

'You told me you were going to the toilet but you were chatting with her,' said Ammamma.

'Who is Nikita?' asked Amma, as she wove her way through the impossible traffic in their small red Maruti.

'I didn't chat with her!' Aman said, surprised. 'I was in the toilet the whole time.'

'For fifteen minutes?!'

'Eww ... who times people when they are in the toilet?'

'I do,' said Ammamma primly. 'It reveals a lot about the state of your bowels.'

'Eww,' said Aman again. 'Anyway, I DID NOT talk to her.'

Ammamma giggled. 'Nigitha is a nice girl. Do you know, she lives in Chennai, too. Her house is in Besant Nagar.'

'OK Ammamma. I will go there tomorrow and marry her. Fine?'

'What on earth are you two going on about?!' asked Amma, irritated by the exchange. 'Would one of you mind telling me?'

'She's the airhostess,' said Aman and Ammamma together.

'Aman has a crush on her,' Ammamma continued.

'I do NOT,' said Aman, flustered. God, why was his Ammamma so embarrassing? Why couldn't she be a normal Ammamma whose hobby was to watch TV soaps and write 'Aum' in her diary?

'Aman was talking to Nigitha and laughing also,' Ammamma said, undaunted.

'She wasn't even there when I went to the toilet. She was serving food somewhere in the front, don't you remember?'

'I took a picture,' said Ammamma. 'Of the two of you.'

'Where? Show me!' challenged Aman. He knew Ammamma was bluffing. Because he was telling the truth, dammit. He'd been holding on till Nikita went to the other end of the plane so she wouldn't know he was inside the toilet for so long. It must be that chicken puff he'd eaten at the airport. It had tasted strange from the first bite but he'd eaten it anyway.

Ammamma took out her iPhone.

'Here,' she said. 'See?'

Aman wondered for a moment if he'd gone crazy. Because Ammamma was right. There he was, chatting with Nikita. They were laughing about something. Maybe he'd cracked a really good joke. Aman felt oddly proud of himself. Then he shook his head. No, this couldn't be real!

'When did you learn to morph pictures?' he asked Ammamma.

Ammamma laughed.

'Why are you talking like a politician?'

'Because I'm wearing different clothes in this picture, can't you see? Not what I'm wearing now.'

Ammamma looked at the picture again.

'That is true,' she said slowly. 'That didn't strike me. How strange. Did you change in the toilet?'

'Ammamma!' exclaimed Aman, exasperated. 'Stop joking and tell me how you did it.'

'I didn't do anything!' said Ammamma. Aman turned to look at her and suddenly, he knew it was true. Ammamma was not making this up. She looked scared. And Ammamma was never scared.

'What's going on?' she whispered, shaking the

phone, as if hoping that would explain matters. As if Aman would fall out of that picture and there would only be Nigitha-Nikita left, laughing at a joke nobody had told.

They reached home.

Just then, Ammamma's phone rang.

'Hello?' she said. 'Hello?' Then, she handed over the phone to Aman. 'It's Nigitha,' she said, in a disbelieving voice. 'She wants to talk to you. How did she get this number?'

Aman didn't want to take the phone from Ammamma. He didn't want to talk to Nikita. He had a strange urge to run to his bed and pull a blanket over his head.

'Who is it?' asked Amma. She was still trying to understand what was going on.

'Take it,' said Ammamma, pushing the phone towards Aman. Her silver grey hair was a mess. Suddenly, she looked so old and tired.

Aman took the phone.

'Hello,' he said.

The voice on the other end was like silk. So smooth, so soft.

'Hi Aman,' she said. 'This is Nikita.'

'Yes?' said Aman, trying to sound nonchalant.

'I hope you don't mind. I had to call. I-I got the

number from the airline. Just wanted to tell you that I'm sorry for your loss.'

'What loss?'

'Your grandmother … it was horrible. Something like this has never happened in all the seven years that I've flown.'

'What happened to my grandmother?'

There was silence on the other end.

'Umm. I'm sorry. Is this Aman Vasanth?'

'Yes,' said Aman. 'I am Aman Vasanth.'

'Well, I know you must be really busy … taking care of all the … you know. But I just wanted to tell you that your grandmother was a most special person. I chatted with her for a while when you … when you were in the toilet. And it came as such a shock, you know. To come back and find her like that. We did everything we could.'

'What are you talking about? My grandmother is right here,' Aman yelled into the phone. 'She's right here.'

There was silence on the other end. And then, Nikita disconnected the call.

'What did she say, Aman? What did she say?' asked Ammamma, panicked. She grabbed his hand. Her touch felt like ice.

'She said she'd like to meet us for coffee one day,' said Aman.

'Oh!' said Ammamma. 'What a funny girl. I must help your mother make dinner now.'

Saying so, Ammamma walked towards the kitchen with slow steps. She had arthritis. Aman waited. She walked past the giant mirror that hung in the drawing room. And then, Aman knew.

NIHAL

Chatura Rao

Eleven-year-old Sahir's parents were not coming home until late. He played till dark – the last kid in a park lit by electric lights. He was walking back home now only because he was hungry.

Sahir saw the moon slip behind clouds dark and heavy with rain. A rumble of thunder made him stop and glance fearfully at the sky. Lightning, like the forked tongue of a snake, zigzagged down behind office buildings in the distance. The wind picked up dust and fallen leaves. A storm was coming.

Sahir looked up at the newly uncovered moon. 'It's half-grown and frightened of

everything,' he mumbled as it slipped behind a thundercloud again.

He came up the lift to the floor his apartment was on. He stopped outside his front door, and felt around in his pockets. 'Oh no,' he whispered. He was locked out!

He wondered if he should phone his mother. She was probably in a house down the road with her friends, but he felt uneasy at the thought of her annoyed voice – 'third time this week you've forgotten your key!' She would speak loud enough for Nita and Pari aunty to hear. 'Careless just like your father!'

Sahir pushed the thought of his parents away. They didn't get along and their fights made him want to disappear like the half-grown moon.

A night last week had been worse than earlier nights. They had shouted ugly words and Sahir had heard the sound of an open palm striking something. He'd leaned over his Play Station and tried to shut the world out. But then his father had come out of their bedroom and snatched away the device. He'd shouted, 'Stop living in your own world! *Grow up!*'

Sahir had pressed his hands over his ears and rocked back and forth. *I want to grow up,*

he had chanted in a rage. *I want to grow up into a monster!*

His parents had noticed his distress. They'd made him lie down and go to sleep. He'd woken up much later, in his quiet bedroom, to a glass of juice his mother had left for him along with a note that said - 'Drink up. You'll feel better'. But he hadn't felt better that night nor the next day. He'd felt like his belly was full of crawling worms.

'I'll climb up and get the spare house key,' he decided now. The spare key was usually hidden on the pelmet of the front door. It was high up and out of reach for Sahir, but he had an idea. He climbed on the shoe rack by his front door, and stepped onto the open window sill. He glanced out. The steep drop of twelve floors made him feel horribly sick. He forced his gaze back to the closed front door. Heels balancing on the ledge of the open window, he reached forward and up to the pelmet. Waves of darkness danced crazily before his eyes. Then, close to his ear came a whisper, 'Grow up, *grow up*.' A growl and a low laugh set him gasping with terror. He felt himself fall.

When Sahir came to his senses, he was lying on the tiles outside his front door. The corridor

was quiet except for the lights above him that flickered with a sharp, crackling sound. Then they went out. Sahir slowly sat up, his mouth dry, and squeezed his temples with his fingertips.

What had happened? He'd heard a voice. But how was that possible? There was no one here.

He glanced around. The semi-lit corridor had unfamiliar shadows. Was someone watching him? All of a sudden, the lift doors opened, and there *he* was! His own face, pulled long and grotesque, reflected on the metal plating inside. Distended eyes stared back for seconds before the doors slammed shut and the lift ground up and away.

Sahir's cellphone let out a series of beeps. It was lying by the window sill he'd been standing on. He crawled over and picked it up. It had messages from his mother.

Pulao rice is by the stove.
Do NOT try to heat it.
Don't turn on the gas stove.
There's a bowl of firnee in the fridge.

The messages reminded him that he was ravenously hungry.

He stood up, still dizzy. Not daring to climb

on the window sill again, he pushed at the front door. To his surprise, it swung open. Hadn't he closed the door properly when he'd gone out to play? Or maybe Papa had come home and left the door open accidentally. He *was* often careless!

Sahir let himself in and closed the door behind him. He felt about for the light switch but found only the plug point, the holes of which his fingers slipped into.

His eyes adjusted to the dim light coming through the windows from the streets far below. He walked through the rooms, listening like an animal. No, his father wasn't home. He himself must have left the door open. Sahir had never walked around in the dark but he felt less afraid now than he usually did. Not *less* afraid, but in fact, unafraid.

'I'm grown up … I'm a big boy!' he thought gleefully.

A warm body wound itself about his calves, almost tripping him up. 'Whew, Minty,' Sahir exhaled, recognising the neighbour's cat! She sometimes found her way into their house by leaping across the balconies. He bent down to pet her. She looked up at him, then moved away. 'Hah, you don't recognise the grown-up me?' he

asked in a friendly way, trying to catch her. But she leapt on the window ledge, and watched him unblinkingly. All that Sahir could see of her were eyes like yellow lanterns.

She watched Sahir make his way to the kitchen in the near dark. He picked up a glass from the rack over the water filter. The filter's nozzle dripped softly. He had the sensation of something alien crawling up from the pit of his stomach. It rose up his throat and made him gag. He thought he might be feeling sick with thirst. He drew water from the filter and took a big gulp, but the water tasted strange ... rusty. He rushed into his parents' bathroom and spat it into the sink. By the light that came through the window, he saw it was dark-coloured and juice-thick.

Sahir's hand shook as he felt along the wall for the light switch. His heart beat faster when the seconds passed and his fingers found nothing. Finally, he turned on the display in his phone and in its dull blue light looked at his tongue in the mirror. Two white worms raised their heads. Sahir dropped his phone with a crash. He choked and spat into the sink, washing out his mouth. He raised his head and then he saw ... the hole.

Right below his chest, in the centre of his

body, was a cloud-like, murky opening. As Sahir stared, transfixed, a shadowy hand reached out of it. The hand was attached to an arm with a muscular shoulder. Sahir looked down at his own body. Nothing. He could see the opening and the arm coming out of it only in the mirror. Choking with terror, Sahir darted out into the living room, where the furniture seemed larger than it had ever been. It filled the room so that he could only squeeze his way to the window, through which city lights reflected off the mess of rainclouds as a dim orange glare.

He tried desperately to find the switch to the standing lamp by the window. Perhaps the electricity was back? He was desperate for light! Sahir's fingers found the dangling switch. But when he yanked at it, the rope gave way.

The shadow man had followed him, walking on all fours like a big cat. He had a long tail. Sahir cowered in the corner of the living room. Leaping across the furniture, the creature came to him.

It changed into a boy, a slouching teenager shaped like Sahir, only, his features were flattened and he was pale as if he'd been indoors for years, had hardly seen the light of the sun. He was dressed in Sahir's school uniform – a loose shirt

tucked into full pants. He wore black shoes on his feet. His tie was tight about his neck. His lips curved into a smile that did not reach his eyes. A worm slipped out from the corner of his lips and down his chin and fell to the floor. Another followed in its wake. Sahir fearfully watched as they disappeared under the furniture.

'Who are you?' Sahir asked, shakily.

'Nihal,' it answered in a hollow voice.

'H ... how did you get inside me ...?'

'I've always been inside you.'

'Are you older than me?'

'I *am* the older you. You wanted to grow up, remember?' The creature's low laugh made Sahir's skin crawl.

'I wished ... to grow into a monster that would stop my parents from fighting ...' Sahir whispered.

Nihal grinned.

'But I grew up,' Sahir argued weakly. 'I ... I walked around in the darkness today and wasn't afraid.'

'That was me,' Nihal said. 'I began to form in you the night you made your wish. Give your body up to me!'

'But why?' Sahir cried out.

'Because you can't cope anymore.'

'No, please, I don't want to,' Sahir pleaded. 'I had only asked to grow up.'

'Okay, w ... ell, you get one last chance,' Nihal barred his teeth in the semblance of a grin. 'Do as I say and prove you're grown up enough to live here!'

'I ... I'll prove it ...'

* * *

'Set the pot of pulao on the stove to heat,' Nihal instructed from the kitchen counter where he sat, one ankle propped across the other knee like a grown man.

'But Mamma said —'

'Mamma thinks you're a silly kid!' Nihal hissed.

Sahir understood. He had to do grown-up things now. He placed the pot of pulao on the stove. Then nervously he tried to light the stove, clicking at the lighter with his right hand and turning the stove knob this way and that. Several tries later, Sahir was sweating. He didn't dare give up though the stench of leaking gas was making him choke. Finally, with a hiss, the stove got going. Huge flames licked the sides of the pot. Nihal laughed, but the sound was overridden by a loud miao. Minty had come into

the kitchen, drawn by the smell of food. She came to Sahir and curled her body about his legs, friendly in her old way. Nihal came over on his fours, his long tail swaying. He shifted into his human shape and bent to pet her, but she leapt away. Her fur standing on end, she darted out of the kitchen, yowling.

'Mean kitty,' Nihal murmured, standing up, a blood-red scorpion scurrying off his tongue. 'When I am Sahir, I'll twist your neck and eat you.'

'You won't be me,' Sahir protested, worried.

'Sooner or later, I will,' Nihal replied.

The smell of hot pulao made Sahir hungry now, but he didn't serve himself. He was afraid to go close to the stove's high flame. By its light, strange shadows had filled the kitchen. Sahir felt other presences come to life inside his chest and belly. They jostled to be released into the world. No, no, he thought, trying to force them back down.

He moved to the kitchen door to switch on the light, meaning to somehow break Nihal's spell or send him away, but Nihal was next to him in a trice. His grip was vice-like on Sahir's wrist.

'Don't forget who is boss, here,' he snarled. 'Take the firnee out of the fridge.'

Sahir was too scared to protest. Besides he could smell the pulao beginning to burn.

'I'll turn off the stove first,' he said.

'No, let it burn!' Nihal sneered. 'Take the firnee out of the fridge. Now.'

Sahir took out the bowl, almost dropping it in his nervousness.

'Eat some.' Nihal's pale eyes burned with hunger.

'I don't want to,' Sahir said, afraid.

'Don't be selfish. The ones inside you want it.'

Sahir put a few spoonfuls of the semi-solid rice sweet into his mouth and watched Nihal's mouth and throat move with pleasure. He himself felt no enjoyment, here in the grip of this creature who terrified him.

'Now bring the rest of the firnee and follow me.'

'The pulao is getting scorched,' Sahir protested, weakly.

'Our parents deserve it. This is our way of showing them! Let's go.'

* * *

Back in his parents' bedroom Sahir stood by the bed next to Nihal, the vessel of firnee in his hands.

'Pour it out on their pillows,' Nihal commanded.

'No, I won't!' Sahir cried. 'How can I do such a thing!'

'They need to be taught a lesson for behaving badly. If you can't teach it to them, go down the dark pit and let me have this body. I will be the son they deserve.'

Sahir looked at Nihal, his older, more hateful self, with a sense of horror. He had brought him into this life by wishing to grow up into a monster. And now he was in Nihal's control, barely able to breathe anymore. Should he simply give up and leave, and let Nihal stay? As his mind wavered, choosing, Nihal reached a shadowy hand to his chest. Sahir felt a huge blow, like his heart was exploding. He screamed, dropping the vessel of firnee on the clean sheets. He dropped to his knees, the dimness around him turning to black.

By the living room window, Minty mewed fearfully. She darted out to the balcony and across to her own apartment, braving the rain which was falling hard and fast outside.

Sahir's parents returned a short while later.

'What's that terrible smell?' his father asked,

frowning furiously. 'Did you leave Sahir to heat up his own dinner?!'

'I told him not to touch the stove! Where is he?' Mamma wondered, peering around.

'Sahir!' she called out.

They switched on all the lights and searched the house. Rain had driven in through the open windows and lay in puddles on the floor. They exclaimed at the pulao charred in the blackened pot. In their bedroom they saw the mess of firnee and came upon their son sitting on the floor, leaning against the far wall. He looked up at them.

'Sahir, have you gone mad?' his mother shouted. 'You've totalled the dinner!'

'You're grounded for the next three days,' his father growled, yanking Sahir to his feet. 'Now clean up the mess!'

Without a word, Sahir did as he was told. As he went from window to window mopping up rain water, his father sat on the sofa and his mother at the dining table, busy with their phones.

'Sahir, bring the pot of soup from the kitchen!' his mother instructed.

Her son put down the mop and went into the kitchen. He carefully carried out the pot of soup his mother had left heating on the stove.

He walked up behind her. He raised the pot over her head that was still bent over her phone. Hearing her giggle over a WhatsApp joke, Papa looked up.

'Sahir, STOP!' he shouted as boiling soup gushed down on her head. Their screams hid the words the boy muttered as he stepped calmly back from the table.

'Not Sahir, Papa. It's Nihal. I've arrived.'

Adithi Rao graduated from Smith College, USA, with a degree in Theatre, and returned to India to work as an assistant director on the Hindi film *Satya*. *Shakuntala & Other Timeless Tales from Ancient India* is her first book for children. *Growing Up in Pandupur* is her second. When the Muse comes knocking, Adithi pens the occasional film script, the rights to one of which have been bought by Aamir Khan Productions Ltd. Over the years, her short stories for children have appeared in anthology collections published by Penguin, Scholastic, Puffin and Zubaan. In her free time, Adithi takes long walks and cooks food that her family politely enjoys.

Chatura Rao is an award-winning journalist and an author. Her books for children and adults have been published by leading publishing houses like Penguin, Bloomsbury, Scholastic, Puffin, Ladybird, Young Zubaan and Tulika. Her most recent books are *A Blueprint for Love*, for adults, and *Gone Grandmother*, a picture book for children.

Chatura teaches creative writing to children at Prithvi Theatre, Mumbai, in summer. Her world, like her city, is always "Under Construction"!

Former journalist **Lubaina Bandukwala** turned into a children's writer (books published by Pratham, FunOK Please) and editor (Time Life, TOI, DNA, Scholastic India) for a simple reason. Now she can read as many children's books as she likes and call it grown-up work!

And because guilty pleasures must be shared, she also curates children's literature sessions at the prestigious Kala Ghoda Arts Festival in Mumbai and has founded her own Children's Literature Festivals – Peek A Book and Fully Booked (with First Mum's Club and Kids Club). This so that children and parents can explore the fabulous world of children's books, especially those produced by Indian publishers – and discover the joys of reading.

Payal Dhar has written books for young adults, and short stories for both big and little people. She's also a freelance editor and writer, and writes on computers, technology, books, reading, games, travel and anything else that catches her interest. When nobody's looking, she either has her nose in a book, is surfing the Net, or battling evil in a computer game. Visit Writeside.net to find out more about Payal's work and play.

Shabnam Minwalla has spent most of her life with words— editing her school magazine, working as a journalist with the *Times of India* and writing non-fiction, for example, a coffee-table book on her beloved alma mater, St Xavier's College.

At the moment she writes food columns, book reviews and features for newspapers and magazines. But what she most enjoys is writing books for children.

Her first book, *The Six Spellmakers of Dorabji Street*, was critically acclaimed and won the Rivokids Parents' and Kids' Choice Awards. Her second book, *The Strange Haunting of Model High School*, has been published by Scholastic. *The Shy Supergirl* and *Lucky Girl*, both published by Duckbill, are popular with young readers.

A new book—a fantasy clue-hunt in Mumbai—is to be published by HarperCollins at the end of 2017.

Sowmya Rajendran has written books for children of all age groups, from picture books for the very young to young adult fiction. She was awarded the Sahitya Akademi's Bal Sahitya Puraskar for her novel *Mayil Will Not Be Quiet* in 2015. Sowmya currently works with *The News Minute*, writing on gender, culture, and cinema. She lives in Pune.